*Amber Pash
on Pink*

Pauline Luke was raised in the central Victorian city of Bendigo, lived for several years in Vancouver, Canada where her two sons were born. She now lives in Melbourne with her husband and White West Highland Terrier Piper.

After graduating from Monash University with a double major in English literature and General and comparative literature she studied Professional and Creative Writing and Editing at RMIT. Pauline works as a freelance editor and has several non fiction books published. Unlike Rebecca's mother she really enjoys cooking.

Amber Pash on Pink

Pauline Luke

UQP

First published 2004 by University of Queensland Press
Box 6042, St Lucia, Queensland 4067 Australia

www.uqp.uq.edu.au

Typeset by University of Queensland Press
Illustrations by Michelle Herzig
Printed in Australia by McPherson's Printing Group

Distributed in the USA and Canada by
International Specialized Books Services, Inc.,
5824 N.E. Hassalo Street, Portland, Oregon 97213–3640

This project has been assisted by
the Commonwealth Government through
the Australia Council, its arts funding
and advisory body.

Cataloguing in Publication Data
National Library of Australia

Luke, Pauline.
  Amber, pash on pink

  For secondary students aged 12–15 years
  1. Teenage girls — Juvenile fiction. I Title.

A823.4

ISBN 0 7022 3428 1

To David and Glenn
who are soo *cool*

My thanks to Hazel Edwards under whose guidance the first draft of this book was written, Anna Barnes who put me right, when I got it wrong, Mark Zocchi & David Treweek for their encouragement, Leonie Tyle for her skilled editorial assistance and enthusiasm, Sarah Madders for her stylish cover and Michelle Herzig for her delightful illustrations.

But most specially to my friends and fellow writers Julie Capaldo and Margaret Geddes, together we have worked our way through rough drafts and rough patches, shared meals and fed each other ideas, discussed the meaning of words and life, and Jack Luke who is constant in his love and his support for all things I do.

Without their help, it wouldn't have happened.

Tuesday 30th January

Would you believe! Only this morning I was thinking about taking up knitting. Really, truly and cross my heart, seriously, thinking that my life was so horrible and so boring that the only thing left for me was knitting. When I tried to tell my mother how horrible and boring my life was, all she said was, 'For goodness sake, Rebecca, there are thousands of people who would gladly change places with you. Instead of feeling sorry for yourself, you should think about them. Better still, do something positive about helping those less fortunate than yourself.'

Well, when you're not a famous rock star who can give a concert to raise funds for all those people less fortunate than yourself, or when your father isn't a wealthy business tycoon who will give you a packet of money so you can set up a charitable organisation, or when you haven't won the lottery because you can't even afford to buy a ticket, your options are pretty limited. Then I remembered how Grandma is always knitting up scraps of wool for the Red Cross, so I decided that's what I'd do. Knit scarves and socks for the poor people. As I'd have nothing else to do in my life but knit, I'd be able to produce hundreds of thousands of socks and scarves. I'd knit so many I'd probably become famous for making all this stuff for the less fortunate and I might get a Dame-hood or a Lady-hood from the Queen, and after I was dead the Pope would probably decide I should be made a saint.

I was getting on the bus, wondering whether being known

as Saint Rebecca, patron saint of souls with cold feet and stiff necks, was all that cool, when I saw him. Drop Dead Gorgeous with blonde hair, blue eyes and a knock-out smile. The moment I looked at him I felt all squishy inside and I just knew he was *The One*.

Couldn't wait to ring Amber and tell her all about him. She said she was really pleased that my life looked like taking a turn for the better. Then, even though Amber is my very best friend and all that, she lost the plot. While I was still telling her about how gorgeous *he* is, she got on to worrying about all those people who wouldn't have nice warm socks and scarves now that I mightn't have so much time for knitting.

Now I'm trying to decide whether I should donate the $3.85 I was going to use to buy knitting needles to charity or put it towards a pot of Pash on Pink lip gloss.

From: 'Rebecca' rlarking@hotmail.com
To: 'Amber' am-chatting@hotmail.com
Subject: Drop Dead Gorgeous!
Date: Wednesday 31st January

Good news! god has obviously decided that my life has been horrible and boring long enough and that it's time to beam a little sunshine in my direction. The *Drop Dead Gorgeous One* was on the bus again tonight, so he definitely must live out my way. (Note that I didn't spell god with a capital G, which means I'm not referring to the real God. That would be blasphemy and could result in a plague of pimples and a year of bad hair days and flaking fingernails.)

Knew I had to be cool and not go panting after him like some wet Year 7, so acted all casual like — looked around as if I wasn't sure where I would sit, then pretended I just happened to notice that there wasn't anyone in the seat next to him. Was about to move in when I copped an elbow in the ribs. Who else but Frances Anne Joppa! By the time I'd caught my breath she had pushed past and was asking, 'Is that seat taken?' in that prissy little voice of hers. That girl has got to be *the* biggest pain in the entire universe.

PS Did I tell you he looks like Shane from *Life in Double Vale* — he is *soo* hot.

From: 'Rebecca' rlarking@hotmail.com
To: 'Amber' am-chatting@hotmail.com
Subject: Frog Face
Date: Friday 2nd February

Amber, you won't believe what Frog Face has gone and done this time! He went and told that new teacher — Mr Weston — that Miss Featherston, our next-door neighbour, was really old and had Alzheimer's. Asked if the Year 7s could do some gardening and paint her fence as part of their community services project. Well, there's not a blade of grass out of place in Miss Featherston's garden, but what Frog Face did was give Mr Weston *our* address. Somehow he'd managed to con his mates into going along with it. Frances Anne Joppa heard about it and blabbed to her mother, and you know what Mrs Joppa's like — she dobbed Frog Face in to Mr Weston. Told him she felt obliged to report the matter, since if Frog Face got away with such immoral behaviour at his age he could end up living a life of crime. Can you believe that woman! And the way she dresses! I mean, she looks like a middle-aged Barbie doll. Wouldn't you just die if your mother dressed like her!

Mr Weston rang Mum and, even though she made me go out of the room, I could hear her going on about Stephen having difficulty accepting his father moving out and living with someone else. She said she'd make sure he was disciplined. So Frog Face isn't allowed to watch telly for a week. Mr Weston must have been pretty cool. In the end Mum went all stupid and giggly. Saying all this stuff about not being totally decrepit, and how she'd just received a promotion with the publishing firm she works for, and that she's still able to play a mean game of tennis. It was *soo* embarrassing, standing there behind the door listening to her carrying on.

I'd better go before she comes in and starts up about wasting time on the net instead of getting stuck into my homework. See ya!

From: 'Rebecca' rlarking@hotmail.com
To: 'Amber' am-chatting@hotmail.com
Subject: Wild weekend — not!
Date: Sunday 4th February

Hi Amber, how was your weekend at the beach? Hope your mother didn't make you spend half the time studying.

Staying over with Dad, Gloria and the Kid is usually about as exciting as watching a goldfish doing laps, but this weekend they picked up a new car. It's really cool. A Falcon. Dark metallic blue with this amazing burgundy velour upholstery. When we were leaving to pick up Frog Face from swimming, Gloria started flapping around, giving us extra towels and telling Dad, 'Make sure Stephen doesn't sit on the seat in wet bathers. The chlorine could stain the fabric.'

I muttered, just loud enough for her to hear, 'If it's going to stress you out so much, why don't you go and swap cars with Mum! Wet bathers on the upholstery aren't a problem when all you drive is a beat-up old station wagon with cracked vinyl seats.'

Well! Gloria just *had* to give this hurt little gasp, which made Dad ask what I had said. Before I could answer, she said, 'Nothing, John, it was nothing,' so he knew straightaway I'd said something to upset her. She's such a cow. Even if I'd met her before Dad went off with her I reckon I still would have thought she was a cow. I just don't know what Dad sees in her. When I asked Mum, she said, 'Beats me, Rebecca. I guess our Gloria must have hidden talents.' I think Mum reckons it's the sex, which is so disgusting.

Gotta go. *Life in Double Vale* is about to start, and wouldn't you know, Mum caved in and is letting Frog Face watch telly again. He told her that the only reason he tried to pull that community service stunt was so the place would look nice for her. Then he carried on about how he missed Dad and all that stuff — he can be such a suck sometimes. (Although I must admit I'm a bit sorry the con didn't come off. The place looks awful now Dad isn't about. Weeds everywhere, the lawn needs cutting and the fence really does need painting.)

See ya tomorrow.

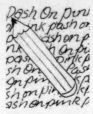

Monday 5th February

Sometimes I get really peed off about the way Mum lets Steve get away with things because of what's happened with her and Dad. When I said, 'I miss Dad too, you know,' she said, 'Of course you do, Rebecca. It's just that Stephen's at an age when a boy needs a father. Besides, you're older and understand better.' But I don't understand. Deep inside I can't help wondering why Dad went off to live with Gloria and the Kid. If he really loves Steve and me like he says he does, why didn't he and Mum just work things out so we could all stay together? Even though Mum and I sometimes have these fights, I really do love her and couldn't bear not to be with her, but I just wish we could be a proper family like we used to be.

Amber says she knows exactly how I feel, but I don't think she really does. She's just trying to be nice because she's my very best friend.

Sometimes when I am walking
along our street
in the misty dampness of early evening
I see a leaf falling
and I remember it was autumn
when my father left
and I feel as though I am falling too.

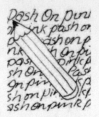

When Amber and I came out of school yesterday, Gavin Spears from 9B was slouched up against the gate. I was racing to make sure I caught the same bus as the *Drop Dead Gorgeous One*, but Amber hung back to talk to him. Mum was hogging the computer doing stuff for work all last night so I had to wait until this morning to find out what happened.

'What's with that Gavin Spears?' I asked.

She acted all casual like, and said, 'Oh, he just walked some of the way home with me.'

'I don't believe it,' I said. 'That guy is such a bogan! Don't tell me he was trying to chat you up?'

She went all splotchy pink around the ears and said, 'No!' but after a minute added, 'Did you know he can play guitar and keyboard as well as the clarinet?'

'Well, there you go, a bogan with culture.' I couldn't believe that my very best friend would be going all splotchy pink around the ears over someone like Gavin Bogan Spears.

'Come on, Bec,' she said, 'he's nice when you get to talk to him. Really he is.'

When I said, 'You're getting the hots for him, aren't you?' she said, 'Don't be stupid.' But by this time all the splotchy pink bits had joined up to make one big red patch that went all the way from her ears to the edge of her nose, so I know it's true.

From: 'Rebecca' rlarking@hotmail.com

To: 'Amber' am-chatting@hotmail.com

Subject: Drop Dead Gorgeous

Date: Friday 9th February

Amber! I found out *his* name. Saw Frances Anne Joppa talking to him at lunchtime and when I got on the bus she was already perched on the seat where he usually sits. 'That seat's taken,' she said, as I plopped myself next to her.

I said, 'That's right, Frances, I've just taken it.'

Reckon she'd spent ages pouffing up her hair and had been double-dipping in the mascara because her eyelashes looked like a barbed-wire fence. She was about to give me a shove when the *Drop Dead Gorgeous One* got on. Well, she immediately turned into little Miss Sunny Bum and as he walked past said, 'Hi Luke,' all wet and soppy like.

'Who's the new boy?' I asked.

'What's it to you?'

'Nothing, but it could be grievous bodily damage to you if you don't tell me.'

'If you must know,' she said in that stuck-up little voice of hers, 'his name's Luke Weston. His father is the new Year 7 co-ordinator. But I wouldn't bother setting your big brown eyes in his direction if I were you. He happened to tell me the other day that he liked girls who had a few brains, so that cuts you out.'

The cow! Just because she gets top marks and beats me in every subject except English she thinks she's Einstein's daughter.

Gotta go, Mum's coming.

Bye.

There's a girl called Frances Anne Joppa
Who's got bulgy eyes like a grasshopper
She's so good and pure
I'd like to find a pile of manure
And into the middle drop 'er.

Thursday 15th February

When I got home from netball, there was Mum, sitting in front of the telly, drinking coffee and getting stuck into the Tim Tams.

'Well!' I said, looking at the packet of Tim Tams and then giving her a meaningful stare.

'Well, what?' she said trying the all innocent bit.

'You *do* know it's the 15th of Feb. today? (My mother said she couldn't start her New Year's resolutions to eat more healthy food and lose weight before the 15th of February because she wouldn't have eaten all the boxes of chocolates and tins of biscuits people had given her for Christmas until then, and not to eat them would be plain bad manners.)

'It's like this, Rebecca,' she said. 'I've been looking at photos of all those emaciated models and film stars recently and I've decided they really aren't the least bit attractive, so I've done a bit of readjustment on the resolutions. In fact, you could say I've made a couple of major life decisions.'

'Oh yeah!' I said, reaching for a Tim Tam before they all disappeared.

'First of all I'm going to accept and make the most of the person I am — which is certainly not some bosomless bimbo. And secondly, I've decided it's time for me to get a new life.'

'Sounds good,' I said, before biting into the biscuit, and as all that yummy chocolate stuff melted in my mouth I told myself that I was going to get a new life too and at the very centre was going to be a certain drop dead gorgeous guy by the name of Luke Weston.

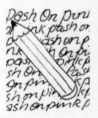

Sunday 18th February

Dad took Frog Face, the Kid and me to the Sunday market. It was great. He let us buy one thing each. Frog Face picked out a leather belt with a Harley Davidson buckle, the Kid got a little silver dolphin balancing a crystal ball on its nose, and I chose this really gorgeous skirt. It's all floaty and wafty and dyed different colours. We had hamburgers for lunch and Dad bought each of us a bunch of helium-filled balloons.

Mum doesn't like the skirt and when she saw the balloons she said, 'Typical of your father. More money than sense.' I hate it when she says stuff like that.

I let one of my balloons go. Watched it drift in the sky until it was just a tiny speck, then I couldn't see it at all.

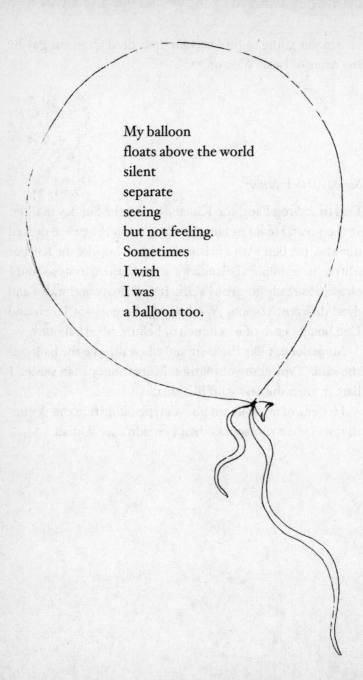

My balloon
floats above the world
silent
separate
seeing
but not feeling.
Sometimes
I wish
I was
a balloon too.

From: 'Rebecca' rlarking@hotmail.com
To: 'Amber' am-chatting@hotmail.com
Subject: Floating Feline
Date: Monday 19th February

Frog Face has really done it this time. He's in *huge* trouble.

You know how I told you Dad bought us those helium balloons? Frog Face tied them to Mum's shopping basket, put Miss Featherston's cat, Napoleon, in the basket and tried to get the basket to float. When Miss Featherston found out she came screaming around to Mum. Reckoned Frog Face was a delinquent and if Mum couldn't control him he should be put in a home. That woman is such an old bat. Anyway, that made Mum real mad. She told Miss Featherston she was overreacting and Stephen would never hurt any animal. Then she said, 'I'd like you to know that Stephen put my best velvet cushion in the basket to make sure Napoleon was comfortable. *And* he tied a piece of rope to the basket, so I doubt it would have floated over the fence, Miss Featherston, let alone all the way to China. Besides, from what I heard, Napoleon quite enjoyed the experience.'

Frog Face isn't allowed to watch telly for a week.

I'd better go. It's my turn to cook dinner. I'm going to make my spag and meat sauce. It's just brilliant. Frog Face usually has about six helpings.

See ya.

Rebecca's Brilliant Spaghetti and Meat Sauce

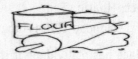

1 onion, chopped (or half a cup of frozen diced onion)

1 clove garlic, smashed (if using the minced garlic in a jar, 1 teaspoonful)

1/2 kilo mince meat (not the fatty stuff)

1 450 gram tin tomato soup (don't add any milk or water)

3 teaspoons Worcestershire sauce

1 teaspoon paprika

1 teaspoon cayenne pepper

1 dessertspoon olive oil

salt and pepper

Heat the oil in a saucepan. Add the onion and garlic and cook until just golden.

Add the meat, about a quarter of it at a time, and brown.

Stir in the can of tomato soup.

Add the Worcestershire sauce, paprika and cayenne pepper.

Simmer on a very low heat for about 45 minutes.

Add salt and pepper to taste.

Serve on cooked spaghetti and top with grated cheese.

Yum-eee!

(Remember to add about 1 teaspoon of oil as well as some salt to the water when cooking the spaghetti.)

Tuesday 20th February

Decided it was time to take some postive action on Luke Weston, so Amber and I have worked out this absolutely brilliant plan to make sure *I* get to sit next to him on the bus tomorrow night. Spent the entire day dreaming up lots of highly intelligent and brilliantly witty stuff to talk about.

Wednesday 21st February

YES! YES! It worked!

At the end of class Amber and I sauntered into the locker room all casual like. Then Amber, who was pretending that she didn't know that the Grasshopper was there, said, 'Rebecca, make sure you catch the later bus. Luke Weston is on library duty and ...' At that point I did this big act, nudging her and saying, 'Ssshshh,' like I was trying to shut her up. Well, zap, zap. As if by magic, one Grasshopper, who was grabbing things out of her locker flat out in order to be first to the bus, turned into a snail. Then, even if I say so myself, my next performance put me right up there with Nicole Kidman. I clapped my hand to my head and said, 'Oh darn! I've left my good pen in the science room. I'd better go and get it before someone pinches it,' and raced out, caught the early bus and got the seat next to Luke.

All day I'd been imagining how impressed he'd be with all the highly intelligent and brilliantly witty stuff I would talk about. He'd be so impressed he wouldn't even notice that I was getting this huge pimple on my chin. But when he smiled at me and said, 'Hi there,' my mouth filled up with saliva and I felt like I was drowning. All I could do was make this senseless 'Guggle glug' sound. Luke didn't seem to notice though, and after a bit he asked which form I was in, then I asked him which form he was in (which of course I knew already). After that there was this horrible silence while I furiously tried to remember some of the intelligent and witty stuff I'd been rehearsing in my mind. Finally, he said, 'How's the netball going?'

'How do you know I play netball?' I said, trying not to sound pleased that he knew.

'Oh, I noticed you wearing your netball uniform the other day.'

Yep, that's what he said. He *noticed* me in my netball uniform the other day. Can't wait to tell Amber.

Thursday 22nd February

Amber was in a really bad mood today. She said it was because her mother was already nagging her about the need to get good grades this year, but I reckon it was because she saw Gavin talking to Anna Barnes, that really pretty girl from 8C.

When I told her how Luke said he had *noticed* me in my netball uniform, instead of being pleased for me all she said was, 'Well, he could hardly miss you, could he? I mean to say, black sports dresses with bright yellow stripes. We look like a bunch of bumble bees.'

'It's a swarm of bumble bees,' I said crossly.

I couldn't believe she'd be so uncaring. There's no way I'd get all cranky with my best friend just because I saw some stupid boy talking to another girl.

From: 'Rebecca' rlarking@hotmail.com
To: 'Amber' am-chatting@hotmail.com
Subject: Wipe-out
Date: Monday 5th March

Amber, you just won't believe what happened on the bus this afternoon!

Luke Weston got on, looked around, smiled, and I just know that when he saw the vacant seat next to mine he was going to come and sit next to me. Then that Chris Asti from 9D came crashing past and flopped himself down beside me.

'Your lucky day today, Rebecca,' he said with that stupid grin of his.

I gave him my 'freeze and drop' look, but that didn't stop him. He just slouched back in the seat and started telling me all about surfing. How awesome it is, the names of all the best surf beaches and how he reckons he's got a pretty good chance of winning the junior surfing championship. He's just so up himself. Then he stretched his arms up in the air like he was doing this great big yawn and dropped them down so one arm was resting along the back of the seat, sort of on my shoulders. I said, 'That move is so old.' (Mum once told me that when she and Dad first went out together that's what he did.) You would have thought that Mr Chris Asti might have had the decency to look just a teensy bit embarassed, but oh no, he just gives this stupid grin and says, 'Yeah, got it from my Dad — an oldie but a goodie.'

Had to sit there and listen to him rave on about surfing. I tell you, if his brain was as big as his ego he'd be a bloody genius.

Then he said, 'You should come and try it some time, Rebecca. I reckon you'd be pretty good — with a bit of personal coaching, of course. I'll tell you what, I'll take you next weekend.'

Before I had a chance to tell him to get lost, that there was no way I was going surfing, let alone with him, he said, 'Looks like my stop coming up,' and bounded off the bus.

Can you believe it? I get stuck with a date to go surfing with Chris Asti, while Frances Ann Joppa gets to sit next to Luke Weston. I could just die of disappointment.

Can't believe you've finished your English assignment already. Next you'll be telling me the Grasshopper is your role model — just joking! I'd better go and get stuck into mine before Mum starts checking up on me.

See ya tomorrow.

Today is happiness.
Today Luke Weston smiled at me.

From: 'Rebecca' rlarking@hotmail.com
To: 'Amber' am-chatting@hotmail.com
Subject: Retail therapy
Date: Wednesday 7th March

I think I'm being punished for spending the $3.85 on Pash on Pink lip gloss instead of donating it to charity. The very day the Grasshopper was away sick and I had the chance to grab a seat next to Luke Weston, Mum picked me up after school so we could go to Mullun Mall to check out the sales.

Mum's always on the look-out for the bargains nowadays. She got a new suit for work for less than half price and we managed to get the sneakers I needed for netball. Last season's style, of course, with awful purple and red stripes, but they were 40% off. I didn't mind about the sneakers so much, because I managed to talk Mum into buying me these absolutely gorgeous two-piece emerald-green bathers that were marked down too. Mum said, 'Well, I've blown the credit card now, so I may as well do it properly.' We picked up a couple of really cool tee-shirts and a windcheater for Frog Face.

From: 'Rebecca' rlarking@hotmail.com
To: 'Amber' am-chatting@hotmail.com
Subject: Hot date — not!
Date: Friday 9th March

Excitement unlimited coming up tomorrow. The big surfing date with Chris Asti. I was going to pretend I'd forgotten about it, but Mum heard about it on the spy vine — someone from that tennis club of hers, I bet.

'Rebecca,' she said, 'you didn't tell me that that nice Chris Asti is taking you surfing on Saturday.'

'That's because I'm not going,' I told her.

'Not going?' she said, looking at me like I'd just confessed to being a serial killer.

'Yeah, that's right. I'm not going because Chris Asti is an opinionated dork. Besides, I didn't definitely say that I'd go with him.'

Then she said, 'I realise you're old enough to make most of your own decisions, Rebecca, but I hope that you'll do the right thing.' And she used the sort of voice that lets you know that if you don't do the 'right thing' she's going to make your life a misery for the rest of the week. So I decided that half a day of Chris Asti is better than a week of my mother's sighs and 'I've always tried to bring you up to be a caring, thoughtful person — where have I failed?' routine.

Better go now. Gotta have an early night so I can get my beauty sleep — ha ha!

See ya.

Saturday 10th March

Even though I was only going out with Chris Asti I decided I'd better wear my groovy new bathers. You just never know who you might see on the beach — or more to the point, who might see you!

Well, I needn't have bothered. When we arrived at Surfers' Point, he dragged this mouldy looking black wetsuit with purple and orange stripes out of his bag and handed it to me.

When I told him, 'I'm not wearing that thing!' he said, 'Sorry, Rebecca, it's the only one I could borrow that was your size, and if you don't wear a wetsuit you'll be frozen within minutes.'

I usually take half an hour to get into the water, but I hit the waves before anyone had the chance to see me. So much for the groovy new bathers!

Must admit Chris was really cool about explaining how to position my feet and balance my weight on the board. I even managed to catch a few little waves before the afternoon was over.

We were coming out of the water when it happened. He bent over and kissed me. It wasn't terribly romantic. I was standing waist-deep in water, turning blue with cold, my hair was blowing across my face and in my mouth, and his lips were all salty and sandy. I must have looked really surprised, because he said, 'What's the matter? Not saving yourself for Luke Weston, are you?'

I said, 'No, of course not.'

Then he said, 'I'm glad,' and kissed me again.

That time it was really good. But not as good as if it had been Luke Weston.

From: 'Rebecca' rlarking@hotmail.com
To: 'Amber' am-chatting@hotmail.com
Subject: Mobile
Date: Sunday 25th March

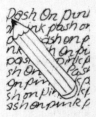

Guess what! Dad bought us a mobile. Not any old mobile, but one of those whizz-bang models that you send photos on. Dad said he wanted us to have it as a security thing for when we go out in the evening to netball or footy practice. We're supposed to share it, but getting it out of Frog Face's grimy little paws is going to be like getting chewing gum off the sole of your shoe.

Of course, Mum just had to go and spoil it by saying, 'It's alright for him, handing out mobile phones, but how does he think I'm going to pay for the calls?' When Frog Face told her it was on a prepaid plan, all she said was, 'It must be nice to be in the position to be able to buy people expensive gifts whenever you feel like it.'

Sometimes I hate all of them.

Friday, 6th April

School holidays. Everybody is doing really cool stuff, except for Frog Face and me.

We have to go to Grandma and Grandad's for the two weeks because Dad is away on a business trip and Mum can't get time off work. Whenever we want to do something like staying at home by ourselves, Mum always says, 'You aren't old enough,' but whenever she wants us to do something like jobs around the house, she tells us, 'You need to become a lot more responsible.'

Worst of all, it means that the Grasshopper will have two whole weeks to chat up Luke Weston.

Thursday 12th April

Dear Mum

Grandma and Grandad were waiting for us at the station. You wouldn't believe what Grandad looked like. It was soo embarrassing. He was wearing a daggy green tracksuit, a bottle-green skivvy, a green woollen beanie and his fluorescent lime-green runners. When I asked him if it was St Patrick's day, all he said was, 'No, Rebecca, it's Wednesday.'

Grandma raised her eyebrows, rolled her eyes and said, 'Your grandfather is into colour meditation. He concentrates on a different colour each day of the week and Wednesday is the day he focuses on green.'

Every afternoon Grandad goes into the garden, cranks himself into the lotus position, and listens to tapes of this whiney music and meditates. Grandma says, 'He's bloody mad. I wish he'd do something useful like painting the house.' But I know from the way she says it she doesn't really mean it.

Grandma has taken up fly fishing. She's really good.

She's teaching me. We go down to the vegetable patch and practise our casting by trying to land the fly on a particular tomato or bean.
Miss you.
Love and hugs
Rebecca

Wednesday 18th April

Grandad drew this really neat chart showing the seven different chakras for me. He said they're like energy centres in the body and each one has a different colour.

— Violet : Crown Chakra - thought
— Indigo : Brow Chakra - light
— Blue : Throat Chakra - Sound
— Green : Heart Chakra - Air
— Yellow : Solar Plexus Chakra - Fire
— Orange : Abdominal Chakra - Water
— Red : Root Chakra - Earth

Grandad reckons that meditating on colour helps to maintain the emotional and physical balance in our bodies. He says that everyone should meditate for at least twenty minutes a day.

I tried it this afternoon, but instead of emptying my mind of all thought I seemed to be thinking about 600 things at once. Or to be more precise, 600 things about the one thing — Luke Weston — the way the corner of his mouth quivers when he is trying not to laugh, the way his hair curls into the back of his neck, the shape of his hands. Then I got this brilliant idea. Even though it was orange Wednesday I decided that I would concentrate on blue, the colour of Luke Weston's eyes. It sorta worked.

From: 'Rebecca' rlarking@hotmail.com
To: 'Amber' am-chatting@hotmail.com
Subject: Family 'addogtion'
Date: Sunday 22nd April

Hi Amber, Got your postcards. Noosa sounds fab. Can't believe your mother makes you do two hours study every morning. She is just unreal! Glad to hear the lifesavers are gorgeous. After all, you never know when you might need mouth-to-mouth resuscitation!

We've only just got back from Grandma and Grandad's, and guess what! Frog Face has a dog. Grandma and Grandad got it for him. Well, it was mainly Grandad's idea. It was Friday and he was all decked out in red — which didn't look half as weird as the purple he was in on Tuesday — and while he was meditating he got this idea that it would be good for Frog Face to have a dog. He rang Mum to check if it would be okay. She wasn't too keen at first but Grandad talked her around. Told her a dog would help Frog Face develop a sense of responsibility and be good for his emotional well-being. I think it was the sense of responsibility bit that won her.

There were some really cute dogs at the pound, but Frog Face picked out this scrawny-looking black thing with ginger and white patches. One ear is pricked up all the time and the other one flops over his eye. He's got these real long legs which fly out in all directions when he runs, and a 'U' bend in his tail. I ask you, have you ever seen a dog with a 'U' bend in its tail? Well, meet Basil! The ugliest dog in the world. But I must admit he's got nice eyes — sad sort of eyes, but nice.

Wednesday 25th April

It's Amber's birthday tomorrow. Now she's fourteen she's allowed to have her ears pierced, so I bought her these gorgeous silver and turquoise dangly earrings.

Mr and Mrs Satchell said they would take us somewhere special to celebrate, but we're not going until Saturday because Mrs Satchell *never* lets Amber go out during the school week. I reckon it's *soo* mean, making her stay home and do homework on her birthday, as if *one* night off the study would hurt. I told Mum and she said, 'That woman needs to lighten up a bit.' I'm going to do a birthday profile to send Amber. That'll cheer her up.

From:	Rebecca' rlarking@hotmail.com
To:	'Amber' am-chatting@hotmail.com
Subject:	Up close & personal profile of the amazing Amber Satchell
Date:	Thursday 26th April

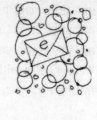

HAPPY BIRTHDAY AMBER

Who is the person you would most like to light your candles?

What is the grooviest present anyone could give you?

If Frances Anne Joppa just happened to give you a birthday present, what do you reckon it would be?

If Gavin Spears gives you a present, what would you like it to be? (Keep it nice!)

Name six people you would most like to come to your birthday party? (Apart from me, of course!)

If you could make a birthday wish that *really* would come true, what would it be?

List five truly wild things you would like to do before your next birthday.

If you could party absolutely anywhere in the world, where would you go?

Which band would you like to play at your party?

If I arranged for you to get a Chinese symbol tattoo for your birthday, what would it say and where would you have it put?

What sort of birthday cake describes you best?

> Chocolate mud cake
>
> Tangy lemon cake
>
> Angel's food cake
>
> Ice-cream cake
>
> Fruit cake
>
> Cream sponge

Friday 27th April

Talk about ear abuse! If having to listen to old Weatherby droning on and on for double maths wasn't mind-numbing enough, I had to put up with Amber's totally out of tune humming all through morning recess and lunchtime. Now Amber is my very best friend and all that, but honestly, when she sings she sounds like a constipated cow. After a while I couldn't stand it any longer and said, 'For goodness sake, Amber, give it a rest. If you're not careful the Grubb Street Boys will have you up for murdering their song.'

'It isn't the Grubb Street Boys,' she said in a really smug Frances Ann Joppa sorta voice. 'It's a song Gavin composed and dedicated to me for my birthday.' Then she started singing.

If listening to stuff like 'Can the light in your eyes see the blush in my heart' wasn't sick-making enough, I had to listen to her rave on about how talented Gavin was, and how Gavin said this and Gavin does that. Then, when she said, 'Gavin understands the stress I'm under because his parents are always putting the pressure on him to get top grades too,' I was totally pissed off. I mean, I am her very best friend and I always agree that her mother is unreal the way she carries on about getting good grades. So I peered at her face and said, 'Do you think they're catching?'

'What?' she asked.

'Those really humungous pimples like I had on my chin the other week, because I think you're getting one on the end of your nose.'

With that she screamed off to the loos to check it out. I guess it was a bit mean of me, but, as Mum says, desperate situations call for desperate measures.

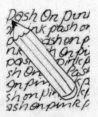

Saturday 28th April

For Amber's birthday celebration Mr and Mrs Satchell took Amber and me to this trendy French restaurant that overlooks Mullun Bay. It was really neat. Instead of cloths there was white paper on the tables and everyone was given a big black crayon so they could write and draw stuff while they were waiting for their meals. Mr Satchell ordered Mullun Fizzers for Amber and me — they look like cocktails but don't have any alcohol in them. We felt *soo* cool drinking from these fancy glasses decorated with little paper umbrellas.

Couldn't believe it when Mrs Satchell ordered the meal in French, even though all the waiters speak English. Next thing this Mr Hobson from Mrs Satchell's work came in, and was he ever a prize geek. He spoke in this *frightfully* posh voice and was wearing a poncy yellow bow tie. While they were talking about all this boring work stuff, Amber and I started to play hangman. Then I heard Mrs Satchell say, 'Well, of course Kevin is a landscape architect.'

Mr Satchell just smiled and said, 'Gardener.'

Mrs Satchell said, 'Landscape gardener.'

Mr Satchell said, 'No, I'm just your common everyday gardener. I have a garden maintenance business, mowing lawns, trimming hedges, that sort of thing.'

When Mr Hobson moved away, Mrs Satchell said, 'How could you embarrass me in front of a colleague like that!'

By then Mr Satchell was starting to get annoyed. 'I'm not ashamed of what I do, Laura. In fact, I get a great deal of satisfaction from my job and I'm very proud of the fact that I've built up the business to the point where I can provide jobs for two other men and a young woman. And I'd also like to remind you that my garden maintenance business helps to provide this family with a very comfortable lifestyle.'

I couldn't believe it. Here it was Amber's birthday and they were arguing. It was *soo* embarrassing.

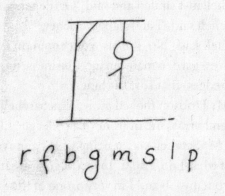

r f b g m s l p

_H__ A D__K H_AD

Sunday 29th April

Frog Face reckons he's going to teach Basil to do all these tricks so he'll get to do ads on the telly. Today he was trying to get him to play dead. There was Frog Face lying on his back with his arms and legs in the air like paws and saying 'Dead Basil, dead' then trying to get Basil to do it. But Basil just sat there with his tongue lolling out and this stupid grinny look on his face. In the end Frog Face rang up Grandad to see if he knew anything about training animals. Grandad said we should get Basil a blue collar because blue is the colour of the throat chakra — the chakra of communication. Mum gave Frog Face an old blue scarf to tie around Bas's neck until we can get to the pet shop to buy him a blue collar. It doesn't seem to be working yet.

When I was talking to Grandad I told him all about Amber's birthday night out and how Mrs Satchell was being all snobby. He said, 'You know, Rebecca, no matter how old we get, the inner-child continues to live within us. That inner-child comes to the surface when adults are enjoying simple pleasures like splashing through puddles or jumping in a pile of leaves or just sitting in the sunshine and listening to the birds. But sometimes the spoilt or boastful part of our inner-child takes control. It sounds to me as if that's what happened with your friend's mother. She may be an adult, but the insecure child in her, the part that needs to feel important, that needs to impress people, took control.'

I told him I thought that Mrs Satchell's child-self shouldn't be allowed out until she could behave.

Monday 30th April

Chris keeps asking me to go surfing with him. I really enjoyed the last time and wouldn't mind going again, but I keep making up all these excuses about why I can't, because I don't want Luke Weston to think Chris and I are an item.

Sometimes I get to sit next to Luke, but whenever I do the Grasshopper always goes and sits in the seat behind or in front of us — the cow!

Mum seems really happy in her new role at work, but some evenings you know she's had a bad day because as soon as she comes in she says, 'Get that dog off the couch.'

If Bas has to get down off the couch he goes from being a

happy dog to all-out miserable and when he has a sad look on his face you feel miserable too, no matter what sort of day you've had.

And Frog Face is always miserable on a Monday because it's my turn to pick what to watch on telly and he never likes the programs I choose.

Why is it that for so much of your life things aren't really bad but they aren't quite the way you'd like them to be either?

From: 'Rebecca' rlarking@hotmail.com
To: 'Amber' am-chatting@hotmail.com
Subject: Grand Slam
Date: Saturday 12th May

Amber, you'll never guess what happened today! Mum beat Frances Anne Joppa's mother at tennis. In the doubles. Isn't it great?

I said to Mum, 'Old Adrian Pervert must have decided to concentrate on the ball instead of your legs for a change.'

Mum flipped me with the tea towel and said, 'I wish you wouldn't talk like that, Rebecca, it sounds so common. But as it happened, Adrian *Purvis* wasn't able to play today. I had a new partner, a very nice man who moved into the area a few months ago.'

She's really pleased with herself. Keeps walking around the house doing all these fancy tennis strokes and saying, 'It takes talent, not flashy clothes, to be a winner.'

Mum told me that Mrs Joppa had on this really gross tennis

outfit. Short, short skirt with a hot-pink satin frill around the hemline, a matching pink satin baseball cap with 'tennis' embroidered on it in silver sequins and hot-pink satin knickers! Wouldn't you just die if your mother dressed like that!

Gotta go. Mum's yelling at me to come and finish the dishes.

See ya.

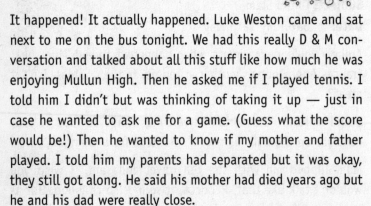

From: 'Rebecca' rlarking@hotmail.com
To: 'Amber' am-chatting@hotmail.com
Subject: D & M with DDG
Date: Monday 14th May

It happened! It actually happened. Luke Weston came and sat next to me on the bus tonight. We had this really D & M conversation and talked about all this stuff like how much he was enjoying Mullun High. Then he asked me if I played tennis. I told him I didn't but was thinking of taking it up — just in case he wanted to ask me for a game. (Guess what the score would be!) Then he wanted to know if my mother and father played. I told him my parents had separated but it was okay, they still got along. He said his mother had died years ago but he and his dad were really close.

You should have seen the look on the Grasshopper's face when she got on the bus and saw Luke sitting next to me. Was she ever cacking herself. Believe it or not, Chris Asti went and sat next to her. You should have seen the act she was putting on, tossing her hair and laughing at everything he was saying with that stupid oinkey oink laugh of hers — not that I cared.

Sunday 20th May

It was Dad's place this weekend. He and Gloria and the Kid have moved into their new house. It's really nice. One of those two-storey places with little windows that poke out from under the roof — dormer windows Dad said they're called.

Gloria was fluffing around looking all hot and nervous when we arrived. When Dad showed us through the place, he made a big thing of telling Frog Face and me how they'd bought a house with four bedrooms so each of us would have a room of our own.

'We've got bedrooms of our own at home,' I said in this real snooty voice. I thought about saying that if he and Gloria hadn't gone off together we wouldn't be needing bedrooms in two different houses. But Dad had this look on his face and his mouth was starting to go all tight and white like it does when he is getting annoyed, so I thought again.

Instead of having dinner in the family room, we ate in the dining room. Gloria had the table set up all fancy with candles and flowers and we had wine glasses instead of ordinary ones for our juice.

'We wanted you to be our first guests in the new dining room,' she said.

Well, she left herself right open there, didn't she? I couldn't help saying, 'We really appreciate being your first *guests*, Gloria.'

Dad said, 'That's not what Gloria meant, Rebecca.' He's

always sticking up for her and saying stuff to try and get us to like her.

We had spaghetti. It was really excellent but I didn't say so.

Finally, Dad asked, 'How do you like the spaghetti? Gloria made it specially, because she knows it's your favourite dish.'

Frog Face was shovelling it in flat out but he said, 'It's not as good as Rebecca's.'

For a moment I thought I could kiss him, but who wants to kiss a frog, especially when it's your brother — and there's no way he's ever going to turn into a prince!

When we got home, Mum asked all these questions about the house and Dad and Gloria. She tries to make out she's not really interested and pretends to be making casual remarks just to be polite, but you know she's just dying to know everything.

I've got an awful headache so I'm going to bed early. I'm not even staying up to watch *Life in DoubleVale*.

Saturday 26th May

Hi Amber!

It's me, Rebecca.

I've got to stay home with Frog Face tonight. Mum's really getting into the tennis. She's decided to play winter comp and has to go to a meeting at the tennis club to sort out some stuff about the teams.

She said we could have Call a Pizza, so do you want to come over?

We'll get a couple of vids and I'll make some of my fabulous frothy coffee — it's just the best.

See you at six.

Bye.

Rebecca's Fab Frothy Coffee
(enough for you and a friend)

Whip a mug full of cold milk until it is really frothy. (The
      calcium-enriched milk is the best. It beats up really well.)
Put the milk in the microwave and heat on high for a minute.
While the milk is heating, put a teaspoon of instant coffee in each
      mug and half fill with boiling water.
Pour most of the heated milk into the mugs with the coffee and
      stir, then top with the last little bit of frothy milk.
Sprinkle with powdered chocolate.

Frog Face uses this recipe to make hot chocolate. He puts a
      handful of marshmallows on top when he's being a real pig
      — which is most of the time.

Thursday 31st May

I'm supposed to be doing a clear-thinking assignment for English. Fat chance! For the past hour Frog Face has been snorting around the house like one of those bulls in that festival in Spain. The Pamplona I think it's called. You see it on telly every year — stupid macho guys running around the streets with raging bulls after them.

Anyway, Frog Face heard there's going to be a dog show next week and decided to enter Basil. When he went to get the entry form, the woman in the office told him she didn't think Basil would be a suitable entrant. The show was for pedigree dogs. Well, that really upset him. As soon as he got home, he came charging into my room and said, 'I reckon Basil is the best dog in the world, don't you?'

'Yeah, Steve, Bas is a great dog,' I said.

Then he went and stormed around some more. Ten minutes later he was back again.

'Look at all the tricks he can do, Bec.' And he made Basil go through his routine, pretending he's got a sore leg, playing dead, begging, dancing on his hind legs — every dog trick you can imagine. I must admit that dog might not be a winner in the looks department, but he certainly is pretty smart.

Just when I finally got started on my clear-thinking exercise, Frog Face was back again. This time he wanted to know if there was an Equal Opportunity Board for animals. He reckoned that Basil was being discriminated against because of his race.

'Race?' I said. 'Dogs don't have a race.'

'No, but they have a breed and that's the same as a race and Basil is being discriminated against because he isn't a pedigree dog,' he said.

'You've just got to accept it, Steve,' I said. 'They want cutsie-looking animals like Gloria's poodle, Bon Bon, in dog shows.'

Well, that shut him up, but by then I was having trouble thinking, let alone thinking clearly.

Think I'll give Amber a ring.

Saturday 2nd June

Caught Mum with her fingers in my pot of Pash on Pink. When I said, 'That's *my* lip gloss!' she said, 'I know it's lip gloss, Rebecca.' (My mother has a way of editing out certain words — like the *my* in front of lip gloss — so that the whole meaning of your sentence changes.)

So, there she was, rubbing *my* Pash on Pink onto her cheeks and telling me, 'Even though it's lip gloss it works really well as a blusher.' Then she turns to me and says, 'I think the colour quite suits me, don't you?'

'I wouldn't think you'd need blusher at all if you're going to be racing around a tennis court all afternoon.'

'That's a point,' she said, frowning into the mirror. Then she got this 'flick on the bright idea' look on her face. 'I know. Just before I go on the court I'll rub some off with a tissue. That way I won't look as pale as a parsnip when I arrive or as red as a beetroot on the court.'

I'm really glad Mum is taking an interest in herself again, but there's something about that tennis club of hers that's a bit of a worry. Last week she was back to colouring her hair, this week it's lip gloss for blusher. I only hope she doesn't start turning out in Pash on Pink lace-trimmed knickers, or sequinned tops. Now I'm trying to decide whether the prospect of my mother becoming a middle-aged Barbie doll, like Frances Anne Joppa's mother, is serious enough to consider sending up a prayer for guidance to capital G god.

From: 'Rebecca' rlarking@hotmail.com
To: 'Amber' am-chatting@hotmail.com
Subject: Best in Show
Date: Sunday 3rd June

Frog Face has done it again! This time he created havoc at the local dog show.

You know how he wanted to enter Basil but couldn't because Bas hasn't got a pedigree? Well, he asked Dad and Gloria if he could take the Kid along to the show. Said he wanted to see what was so special about pedigree dogs. I reckon he had a bit of friendly jeering in mind, but Dad and Gloria thought he was being pretty nice taking the Kid out and all that. Trouble is, he didn't mention he was taking Bon Bon as well — and Bon Bon's on heat, isn't she!

Just as the parade of all the winning dogs started, Bon Bon 'somehow' managed to pull free and went racing across the oval, thirty pedigree dogs in *hot* pursuit. (Pretty good pun, hey?)

Mr Pauser, the president of the Pedigree Dog Owners' Association, lunged out and tried to grab Bon Bon's leash as she went racing by, but he slipped and fell into this huge puddle. The woman who had told Frog Face that Basil couldn't be entered in the show got all splattered with mud. She was so busy screeching 'Look at my new pink suit, it's ruined!' that she didn't see the Great Dane coming in her direction at 100 kilometres an hour. She got bowled over, sending Mr Pauser — who had just managed to scramble to his feet — flying face-first into the mud again.

Bon Bon headed for the car park and there were dogs and people running in every direction as she kept dashing between cars and four-wheel drives. They finally found her in the back seat of a Range Rover with what Frog Face described as 'a really cool-looking cocker spaniel'. We reckon there's a chance she could produce a very interesting litter in a few months.

When I told Mum, she said, 'I bet Our Gloria wasn't too pleased.' Mum always manages to say 'Our Gloria' so that it sounds like some dreadful disease.

I think she had a pretty good time at the tennis club dance last night. She was actually singing when she was cleaning out the shower this morning.

'Meet a spunk at the dance, did we?' I asked.

She said, 'Don't be ridiculous, Rebecca.'

But my mother doesn't normally sing when she's doing the housework — particularly when she's cleaning the shower.

Gotta go. The phone's ringing and Mum's yelling at me to answer it because her hands are covered in cleaning stuff.

From: 'Rebecca' rlarking@hotmail.com
To: 'Amber' am-chatting@hotmail.com
Subject: Mum's Birthday Bash
Date: Saturday 9th June

Haven't had the chance to chat earlier.

It's Mum's birthday and Frog Face and I decided we'd make it really special. Frog Face cooked breakfast. Would you believe he put green food-colouring in the scrambled eggs? They looked revolting but Mum said they were the best scrambled eggs she'd ever tasted.

When she said, 'Green! Why, that's the colour of the heart chakra, isn't it?' Frog Face went all red and soppy but looked kinda pleased too. Then he went into his room and brought out this beautiful bunch of roses. Beats me how they weren't all dead. A few hours in his room with the smell of his stinking sneakers and the rotting bones Basil has hidden under the bed is enough to kill off most living things.

I gave her a pot of Seductive Strawberry lip gloss, which is a lot more suitable for someone her age than Pash on Pink. And I made this best-ever chokky cake and put two candles on it. Told Mum that was because she was too old for candles, but she said, 'I thought it was because it was from the two most important people in my life.'

We're taking her to Macca's for tea. Well, it's mostly me that's taking her. Frog Face hasn't had any pocket money for the past two weeks because of the dog show thing.

Gotta fly, Mum's ready to go.

See ya at school tomorrow.

Rebecca's Best-Ever Chokky Cake

1 1/2 cups self-raising flour
pinch of salt
1 cup brown sugar
1/4 cup boiling water
75 grams butter
3 tablespoons cocoa
1 egg
1/2 teaspoon vanilla essence
1/2 cup milk

Sift flour and salt into a bowl then add the brown sugar.
Add cocoa to boiling water, mix into a smooth paste, add butter
     and stir until melted.
Beat egg, milk and vanilla together.
Add cocoa mixture and egg and milk mixture to flour, and mix
     well.
Pour into a greased cake tin.
Bake in a moderate oven 30–35 minutes (Celsius 180–190° /
     Fahrenheit 350–375°).
Let cool for 10 minutes before turning out of tin.
When cool, top with chocolate frosting.

Chocolate frosting
Soften 25 grams of butter. Mix in 1 cup of sifted icing sugar and 1
     tablespoon of sifted cocoa. If necessary, add a little milk to
     get the right consistency.
(You can make different kinds of frosting by leaving out the cocoa
     and adding other things, such as a few drops of peppermint
     essence and green colouring, or some strawberry essence.
     I made orange icing once and that was delicious too.)

From: 'Rebecca' rlarking@hotmail.com
To: 'Amber' am-chatting@hotmail.com
Subject: Takes the prize
Date: Sunday 10th June

Just had the old bat from next door on our doorstep. As soon as Mum answered the door, the old bat flung this certificate that said 'Third Prize — Rose Section' in front of Mum's face and said, 'Just look at this.'

'Why, congratulations, Miss Featherston,' Mum said.

Well, I thought the old girl was going to have a seizure. She went all huffy and blowy and red in the face before she finally managed to splutter out, 'I'll have you know that I've taken off the first prize for roses at the Mullun Horticulture Show for the past five years. The only reason I didn't win this year was because the night before the show someone came and cut off my very best blooms.'

'Really!' said Mum. 'That's most unfortunate. Did you happen to see who did it, Miss Featherston?'

She started to say, 'No, I didn't but ...' when Mum interrupted and said, 'The thought that someone would deliberately sabotage your rose bushes in order to prevent you taking first prize in the show is quite unbelievable. But I can assure you that I'll keep a close watch to make sure that such a thing doesn't happen again.'

Then Mum told Miss Featherston that it was her birthday. I couldn't believe it when she went and said, 'I would be delighted if you would come in for a cup of tea and a piece of the delicious chocolate cake that the children made for me.'

By now the old girl had calmed down and she said, 'I must admit to being rather partial to chocolate cake, Mrs Larking, but unfortunately I can't accept your kind offer, as I've got to go and feed Napoleon.'

Of course, Mum took the hint and insisted on cutting off some cake for her to take home. She gave her this huge piece so there's hardly any left now.

What happened in *Life in Double Vale*? We didn't get to watch TV. Mum said she thought we should do something constructive for a change. She suggested a nice game of Scrabble. Frog Face hates Scrabble but he didn't argue.

Gotta go now.

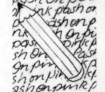

Thursday 14th June

Amber was all upset today. Her mother saw her walking home from school with Gavin last night. Amber said that as soon as she walked in the door her mother went absolutely mental and started yelling, 'I'm not having any daughter of mine being seen with such a scruffy-looking creature. If you want to go walking home with someone, for goodness sake choose someone decent, like one of those nice boys from St Kevin's College.'

Amber said, 'You couldn't believe the way she carried on, Bec!'

Knowing Mrs Satchell, I reckon I could. Even though Gavin isn't one of my favourite people, I don't think Mrs Satchell should go slagging him off just because his shirt is always hanging out and his hair looks like it's been cut by a lawn mower.

From: 'Rebecca' rlarking@hotmail.com
To: 'Amber' am-chatting@hotmail.com
Subject: Hot goss
Date: Sunday 17th June

Amber, you won't believe this. You just won't believe it. Frances Anne Joppa's mother has gone off with that slimy Mr Purvis from the tennis club. Mum just told me. She said, 'Rebecca, I'd like you to be nice to Frances Anne Joppa. She's going through a very difficult time.'

'Nice!' I shrieked. 'She wasn't very nice to me when you and Dad separated. I'm in the locker room crying my eyes out and all Frances Anne Joppa could say was, "You'd better pull yourself together, Rebecca. The relay race is on in five minutes. We need to get at least second place in order to win the Inter-school Sports".'

When I said, 'I'm sorry, but I've got a few problems,' she said, "We've all got problems. Just make sure you're out in front in the last leg of the race".'

Now I'm expected to be *nice* to her. Can you believe it? Sometimes I just don't understand my mother.

Here she comes. I'd better go.

See ya.

Monday 18th June

The stuff about Frances Anne Joppa brought back the feelings I had when Mum and Dad separated. Just when I think I've got everything under control, WHAM, something happens that stirs up all the anger, hurt and sadness.

I couldn't concentrate on my science class. Broke a test tube and spilt sulphur all over the bench. Ms Iser came across to me and said, 'For goodness sake, Rebecca, whatever's the matter with you today?' I told her I had bad period pain. I never get period pain, but I must have looked the right shade of pathetic because it worked. She told me to go outside and get a bit of fresh air.

I headed for the loos — which were even more grotty than usual. One of the cisterns was running non-stop and water was flowing over the toilet bowl into all the other cubicles. There were strips of toilet paper, chocolate-bar wrappers and cigarette butts floating about on the floor. But I thought that at least I'd have some space to sort things out in my mind.

I'd just swung up onto the bench next to the hand basin and was sitting with my back pressed against the mirror when the Grasshopper came in. She gave me a look that clearly said she hated breathing the same air as me, but she looked pretty dreadful so I couldn't help feeling a bit sorry for her.

'Frances,' I said — even though I was feeling sorry for her I still refuse to call her Frances Anne, it's such a plastic name — 'I'm really sorry about your mother going off with that awful Mr Purvis. I know how you must feel.'

'Shut your face,' she yelled. 'You don't know a thing about how I feel, so just shut your face or I'll shut it for you.'

Funny thing is, hearing her talk like that made me feel better. I always thought the Grasshopper was a real jelly baby, always so prim and proper. I even thought she might go to pieces because her mother walked out. But when she yelled at me like that I knew she'd be okay.

Tuesday 19th June

Luke Weston was sitting with his arm around Frances Anne Joppa at lunchtime.

Amber said it was probably because he was feeling sorry for her, but it still made me feel the pits.

On the way home Chris Asti asked me again to go surfing with him on the weekend.

I said, 'You've got to be crazy. No one in their right mind goes surfing this time of the year.'

When he said, 'I do,' I said, 'Well, that just goes to prove my point!'

'If you don't want to go for the real thing, Rebecca,' he

said, 'how about coming to see the new surfing movie, *Wild Waves*, with me?'

I told him I would, as long as we went out as 'just friends'.

'Okay,' he said, 'just friends.'

I was sure I heard him say 'for the moment' under his breath, but when I asked him, he said, 'Me, say that? Sounds like wishful thinking, Rebecca.'

Whenever I begin to think he really is quite nice he goes and says or does something that makes me *soo* mad.

Sunday 24th June

It seems like every time we go to Dad and Gloria's there's some sort of drama, and you can count on Frog Face being at the centre of the action. I was watching telly with Gloria, which is about the smartest thing to do because then she doesn't try to be all caring and sharing by asking questions about school and what I've been doing and all that sort of stuff. And I don't have to be all polite and talk to her. Next thing we heard these awful noises coming from the kitchen. We raced out and there was Frog Face sitting at the table with this bowl of revolting wormy-looking things in front of him. He had his head tipped back and his mouth wide open and he was dropping one of the things into his mouth. The Kid was sitting opposite him, grabbing his stomach and saying, 'Oh yuk,' and making these gagging noises.

Well, Gloria really cracked it. 'You're the most disgusting child I have ever known,' she screamed at Frog Face. Then she swooped up the Kid and began to march out of the kitchen saying that she wouldn't trust Steve alone with the Kid ever again. It was like world war three!

The Kid was bawling, 'I want to be with Stephen, he's my friend.'

Frog Face was yelling, 'You've got no right to call me disgusting.'

Gloria was screaming, 'What else would you call someone who eats worms.'

And Bon Bon was racing around the kitchen table yapping and barking like a mad thing.

Then Dad came storming in and wanted to know what all the commotion was about. Gloria immediately went into her 'You can't imagine what I've had to put up with' routine.

Frog Face started shouting, 'I wasn't eating a bowl of worms. It was just some cooked spaghetti that I'd rolled in cocoa powder, but it seems that *some* people can't take a joke, so I'm out of here.'

Well, that set the Kid off again. He started wailing, 'I don't want Stephen to go away.'

Dad finally managed to get a word in and said, 'I think it might be a good idea if we all go down to the park for a while. We can have a turn on the swings and a kick of the footy and throw a few baskets too.'

As soon as I said I didn't want to go, I realised I'd made a really bad move, because then Gloria said, 'Yes, Rebecca and I will stay behind and start to get the dinner ready.'

In the end everything quietened down and the Kid and Stephen went off with Dad as happy as Batman and Robin. Gloria got it together again and asked if I would like to make the dessert. She showed me how to make this Passionfruit Fluff, which is really excellent.

When I told Mum, she said, 'I've no doubt it is excellent. After all, if anyone knows about *passion* fruit it's sure to be Gloria.'

Gloria's Glorious Passionfruit Fluff

Mix a packet of pineapple or lemon jelly with 1 cup of boiling
water.

Allow to cool but not set.

Beat 1 egg with 1/2 cup sugar until thick and fluffy.

Add 1 cup of milk and the pulp of 6–8 passionfruit (If passionfruit
are not in season, you can use a tin of passionfruit pulp.)

Add the mixture to the jelly, pour it into a lightly greased mould,
and place in the fridge.

When ready to serve, turn the 'fluff' out onto a plate and decorate
with whipped cream.

If you have thoroughly greased the mould — some of that spray
oil is good — it should turn out fairly easily. Just ease the
base of the dessert away from the mould with a knife. If it
doesn't come out, quickly dip the mould into a bowl of hot
water and then turn onto the plate.

From: 'Rebecca' rlarking@hotmail.com
To: 'Amber' am-chatting@hotmail.com
Subject: Death by Embarrassment
Date: Friday 29th June

Amber! I think I'll just die of embarrassment. I found out that the mystery man Mum has been dating is Mr Weston. I can't believe it. I don't know how she could do such a thing to me.

She knows I really like Luke Weston and she's been going out with his father behind my back. And the worst thing is, she doesn't seem to care. All she said was, 'Come on, Rebecca, why the big drama?'

'Drama,' I yelled. 'What sort of a chance will I have of getting it together with Luke Weston when you're crashing onto his father.'

'Rebecca, I am not crashing onto him, as you so colourfully put it. We just happen to have developed a very enjoyable relationship.'

When she said *relationship* I just knew it must be serious. I told her that I could hardly get into a *relationship* with someone who's likely to end up being my brother and she started to laugh. I couldn't believe it. My own mother laughing when my whole life had just exploded into a million pieces.

Thank goodness the holidays start tomorrow. I'd be *soo* embarrassed if I bumped into Luke Weston. And Frances Anne Joppa! Can you imagine what she'd be like?

Gotta start packing, we're going to Dad's tomorrow.

See ya.

Friday 6th July
Dear Amber

How's the holiday going? Any hot ski instructors like the one in Life in Double Vale cutting the slopes?

It has been soo boring here. Big moments were roller-blading on Tuesday and going to the pictures with Gloria and the Kid on Thursday. Don't think I'll be able to cope if it gets any more exciting!

Tomorrow we go to Grandma and Grandad's, which is just as well because Frog Face got himself into big cack today. He and the Kid saw a photo of a poodle with its coat clipped into little balls around its legs and tail and decided to give Bon Bon a trim. I think they must have done the job with nail scissors. She looked really weird. Dad burst out laughing when he saw her and poor old Bon Bon ran and hid under the bed and wouldn't come out. Gloria got all upset and started to cry. She said that no matter how hard she tried we'd never get to like her. I even felt sorry for her — just for a minute.

Make sure you do all the things I'd do — and that sure ain't studying!
Lots of luv
Rebecca

Class of
2012

Saturday 7th July

Grandad picked us up from the station by himself today because Grandma was at home cooking dinner. He was all decked out in yellow and looked like a geriatric canary.

We had the best meal — roast lamb with potatoes and pumpkin and peas and carrots from Grandma's garden, and for dessert she had made this really delicious lemon pudding.

Grandad said, 'You know, the reason I married your grandmother was because she is such a superb cook.'

'Sounds like a better reason than marrying for love,' said Frog Face.

Well, that set Grandad spinning off on one of his lectures. 'English is one of the richest languages in the world,' he said, waving his fork in the air, 'but unfortunately it has only one word to describe a whole range of vastly different emotions. I ask you, how can you compare the love you feel for your wife with a love of chocolate cake? The feeling you have for your country and your fondness for your goldfish? The unshakeable love a parent feels for their child and the pleasure you derive from playing football?'

Then he looked at Frog Face and said, 'Do you understand what I am telling you, Stephen?'

Grandma said, 'If you don't stop flicking gravy all over the clean tablecloth you'll get to understand the meaning of a few more words.'

Grandma's Really Delicious Lemon Pudding

3 tablespoons plain flour, sifted
1 cup sugar
1 tablespoon butter, melted
1 cup milk
2 eggs (separate and beat the egg whites until stiff)
grated rind one lemon
3 tablespoons lemon juice

Mix flour, sugar and lemon rind in a bowl.
Add lemon juice, melted butter, milk and egg yolks.
Fold in the stiffly beaten egg whites.
Pour mixture into a buttered ovenproof dish and place the dish in
    a pan of hot water.
Bake in a moderate oven 45–50 minutes.
Serve with cream or ice-cream (or both if you're a guts like Frog
    Face).

Wednesday 11th July

Dear Mum

Not much happening here. Grandad goes jogging every day and takes Steve with him. You should see them. Steve's pole-vault legs and Grandad's scrawny white legs. Grandad wears daggy purple satin shorts and he's glued a heap of reflectors onto an old red tee-shirt. He says it's so people can see him on the road, but I can't see how anyone could miss him.

Grandma and I went to Little Mia Mia Creek this afternoon. We'd been fishing for about half an hour when I caught a fish. Grandma said it was a trout. I was so excited when I pulled it in, but when I unhooked it and saw the way it was gasping like it was drowning in air I felt really awful. Grandma must have felt the same. She said, 'Such a beautiful creature should be swimming through sunlit waters, not sitting on a dinner plate.'

So we went to the edge of the creek and let the trout slide back into the river again. It stayed in the shallows for a few moments, then gave a flip of its tail like it was waving goodbye, and swam off.

We didn't do any more fishing, just lay back in the grass listening to the sound of the creek running over the stones and watching the clouds changing shapes. Grandma told me the names of the different birds we could see and hear and I told her about Luke Weston and how I'd been really mad at you when I found out you were going out with his father. She reckons it is important that you have someone special in your life too, and that there is no reason I shouldn't have a special friendship with Luke Weston as well.

Instead of fish we had toasted cheese sandwiches and chips for dinner. Frog Face kept making these really pathetic fish jokes, like:

What's the biggest fish in the world?
The one that got away.
When's the best time to go fishing?
Yesterday, because that's when all the big ones were biting.
What did Dick say when Tom told him he cleaned 699 fish in one day?
Now that takes guts!

Grandad's joke was even more pathetic:
Did you hear about the man who went off for a week's fishing?
He didn't catch anything until he got home.
Grandma said, 'Very funny, I don't think.' Then she recited this little fishing poem:
Oh give me the luck to catch a fish
So big that even I
When talking of it afterwards
May have no need to lie.

I reckoned we'd had enough fishy jokes so didn't bother to tell the one about the boy who caught a huge fish with a piece of string and a safety pin. When asked what sort of fish it was, he said, 'I'm not sure, but the bloke sitting next to me on the pier said it was a Bloomin Fluke.'

After dinner we played Monopoly. Boy, is Grandad a sore loser.

Miss you too.

Luv and hugs

Rebecca

Clouds have shapes
that change
like dreams.

Wednesday 18th July

Mum told Frog Face he's got to turn the sound system down a notch or two because Miss Featherston's been complaining about the noise, which is pretty unfair because Frog Face really doesn't have it all that loud. Miss Featherston told Mum that once she used to be able to sit in her garden with Napoleon and enjoy listening to all the tiny sounds of nature.

'The old bat's got it in for me. She moans about everything I do,' Frog Face said. 'Just how quiet would she like it to be?'

'Oh, I'd say quiet enough to hear the snails munching on plants,' Mum said. 'But I think if you turned the music down just a bit, it might keep her happy.'

From: 'Rebecca' rlarking@hotmail.com
To: 'Amber' am-chatting@hotmail.com
Subject: Snail Tales
Date: Thursday 19th July

I reckon Frog Face is getting more like Grandad all the time. Today after school he was out in the garden with a bucket collecting snails. I thought he might be planning to pull another stunt like the worm thing, but he said he's going to relocate them to a more snail-friendly environment.

Just the thought of their slimy little bodies slithering all over the place gives me the creeps. When I asked how he could bear to pick them up, he said, 'All creatures have their place in nature's scheme of things, Bec.' Isn't that such a Grandad thing to say?

Anyway, I wanted to know if you'd be allowed to go to the shopping mall on Saturday. Dad gave me some money to buy a new tee-shirt to go with the jeans Mum bought me last week.

Saturday 21st July

Went to Mullun Mall with Amber this afternoon. Picked out this really gorgeous hot-pink tee-shirt. It was on sale so I had some money left over and got a can of pink hairspray and another pot of Pash on Pink lip gloss too, so it's going to be a totally pink look for me. I was feeling really happy and said to Amber, 'Let's go and have a coke at the Jump 'n Rock Cafe,' but she said she had to meet Gavin at three.

That made me really mad. 'I suppose the only reason you bothered to come shopping with *me* was as a cover-up so your mother wouldn't find out you were meeting *him*.'

Amber said, 'That's not fair, Bec. You know I always love to go shopping with you but I want to see Gavin as well. Anyway, you can come.'

'Oh, sure,' I said. 'Gavin will be really thrilled if I do that.'

Amber tried to tell me he wouldn't mind, but I told her, 'No way, I've got better things to do,' and marched off.

When I got home, Miss Featherston was hanging over the fence talking to Mum.

'What was the old bag whingeing about this time?' I asked when she came in.

Mum said, 'She's really not such a bad old thing, Rebecca. I think she's just lonely, and as it happens she wasn't whingeing about anything. She was simply asking if we had a problem with snails because it seems they've been attacking her garden in plague proportions.' Then Mum said, 'It's odd, isn't it, but I haven't seen a snail in our garden for days.'

'Yeah!' I said. 'Real odd.'

I told Mum about Amber and Gavin Spears. 'I just can't understand why she wants to spend time with *him*. He's such a loser.'

'Don't go calling people losers, Rebecca. It's an awful thing to say about anyone.'

'Loser, moron, stupid git, take your pick.' The last thing I needed was one of Mum's lectures about giving people negative labels.

'This isn't the green-eyed monster talking, is it?' Mum said.

When I wanted to know what she meant, she said, 'Jealousy!'

'Don't be ridiculous. There's no way I'd want to be an item with Gavin Spears.'

'That's not what I mean,' Mum said. 'Are you sure you aren't just a tiny bit jealous because Amber wanted to spend time with him instead of you?'

'No, it's just because he *is* a loser and I can tell he doesn't like me.'

'Well, that's hardly surprising, is it?' Mum said.

'What do you mean?' I shrieked. I couldn't believe it. My

own mother saying she didn't think it surprising that some-one didn't like me.

'Well, it's pretty obvious you don't like him and when someone doesn't like you you're hardly going to think they're the greatest thing since spreadable butter. But sometimes if you make the effort to get to know someone, you discover that they're really quite nice after all.'

'If it's not Stephen sounding all Grandad like, it's you,' I said grumpily.

'Could be worse,' Mum said with a grin. 'After all, you must admit there's certainly no way your grandfather could ever be considered boring. In fact, I'd say he's one of the most colourful senior cits around.'

Sunday 22nd July

When Mum says, 'You wouldn't believe the day I've had at work!'
You know you're going to get takeaway for dinner.

When Frog Face says, 'Have you worn your new jeans yet?'
You know he's hoping you will say he can have the last Tim Tam.

When Dad says, 'You wouldn't believe the month I've had at work!'
You know he's exceeded his sales budget and is about to check out the catalogues.

When Frog Face says, 'I've done all my homework.'
You know he's lying.

When Mum says, 'Purple can be such a difficult colour to wear.'
You know she's seen Gloria in her new coat.

When Miss Featherston says, 'I don't want to complain.'
You know she wants to complain.

When Mum says, 'I guess I'd better clean the oven.'
You know she's hoping you'll say, 'But I wanted you to drive me to the library.'

When Grandma says, 'Just how old does he think he is?'
You know Grandad is trying to do a headstand again.

When Frances Anne Joppa says, 'When's our maths assignment due, Mr Weatherby?'
You know she's already done hers.

When Amber says, 'Have I told you ...'
You know you're going to have to listen to her rave on about Gavin Spears.

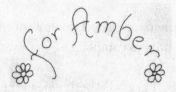

Amber has god a cold in da head
Her node id all runnind
And her eyeds ard all red
I hope she's sood bedder
'Cos I midd her a lot
Amber, da best frienddd
Thad I had got.

Tuesday 24th July
Room 11
Maths 2
Dear Amber

    Mr Weatherby spent the first part of the period droning on with all the usual boring stuff about how an understanding of maths helps to give us an understanding of the world. I was trying to keep my eyes open while my brain had a sleep when I heard him say, 'Because it's most important that students become used to being in "an exam situation", I am going to set a maths test for you every fortnight.'

    Now isn't he all heart!

    You can imagine what the Grasshopper was like, sucking up to him by asking all these questions like, 'How soon can we have the first test, Mr Weatherby? Will our marks count towards the end-of-year results, Mr Weatherby?' She really is something from planet weird.

    Gotta go, he's started to hand out a set of maths exercises and if I don't get started I'll end up with double homework.

Hope you're better soon.

Luv

Rebecca

From: 'Rebecca' rlarking@hotmail.com
To: 'Amber' am-chatting@hotmail.com
Subject: Great news!
Date: Thursday 26th July

Amber, I've got the most amazing bit of news which will help make you feel lots better! After science Ms Iser announced that there's going to be a social for the middle-school students and their families at the end of the year to help raise funds to buy gym equipment for the new leisure centre. Isn't that just excellent! Then she went on and told us that she suggested to the principal that it would be a good idea if the girls asked the boys for a change. She reckons in this day and age it is important for young women to be comfortable about approaching a young man to ask him out. (Of course, you'll never guess which young man I'm going to ask!) Ms Iser also said that she and some of the other teachers are going to organise dancing classes to be held after school on Wednesdays.

What are you going to do if your mother won't let you ask Gavin to be your partner?

Must fly, *Life in Double Vale* is about to start.

See ya.

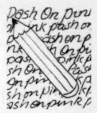

Friday 27th July

Gavin was waiting to see me after school. Wanted to know how Amber was. He said, 'I'd give her a call or go and see her only I don't think Mrs Satchell likes me.' I said, 'I don't think you'd have to be a rocket scientist to work that one out, Gavin.'

He said, 'I guess not,' and ambled off.

Couldn't concentrate on *Life in Double Vale*. Just keep dreaming about the school dance, imagining myself waltzing around in Luke Weston's arms. It's going to be *soo* romantic.

MULLUN SECONDARY COLLEGE

Mullun Secondary College
Sailors Road
Mullun
Friday 27th July

As part of their effort to raise funds to buy gymnasium equipment for our new multi-purpose leisure centre, the Mullun Citizens and Teachers Society is planning to hold several functions in our splendid new facility, including an end-of-year dance for the middle school students and their families, on Saturday 16th December.

Some of the students have requested that the night be formal. However, as the Year 11 Deb dance is traditionally the school's formal occasion, it has been decided to compromise by setting a semi-formal dress code.

The event will be strictly supervised, pass-outs will not be issued, and any student caught smoking or consuming alcohol will face suspension.

Mrs Johns, the secretary of the Mullun CATS, would be pleased to hear from any parents prepared to assist with the catering.

I would encourage all families to support the school in what promises to be a wonderful family event.

G. Andrews
Principal

From: 'Rebecca' rlarking@hotmail.com
To: 'Amber' am-chatting@hotmail.com
Subject: School Dance
Date: Saturday 28th July

What did your mother say when she got the notice about the school dance?

When I said to Mum, 'I reckon it'll do the boys good to find out what it's like, hanging around, hoping that someone will ask you for a date,' she said, 'And I think it will do the girls good to have to ask someone and hoping they won't refuse.'

I wanted to go shopping for my dress during the holidays, but Mum said, 'Don't be ridiculous, Rebecca, we've got plenty of time to do that, the dance isn't till the end of the year. Besides, the sales will be on in a month or so. I'm sure we'll be able to pick up something nice then.' I tried to tell her that by 'then' all that will be left is the drakky stuff that no one else wants. One of these days I'm going to go out and buy exactly what I want, without having to wait for the sales, or having to get stuff from Target or the factory outlets.

I can't believe you're mooning around, being all miserable about not seeing Gavin for a couple of weeks, when you're heading off to Noosa where there's a beach full of spunky surfers to crash on to. All I'll be doing is spending the first week with Dad and Gloria and the second week with Grandma and Grandad, which doesn't even register one on the excitement scale.

Hang on a minute, there's someone at the front door and Mum's in the shower.

It was Miss Featherston again. This time she reckons Frog Face is training Basil to pee on the fence near her rose bushes. I don't know where that woman gets her weird ideas from.

Better go, Mum's yelling for me to check out the dress she's wearing to the tennis club thing. I think she's out to impress!

From: 'Rebecca' rlarking@hotmail.com
To: 'Amber' am-chatting@hotmail.com
Subject: School Dance
Date: Sunday 29th July

Have you told your mother you're going to ask Gavin to the school social yet?

I'm going to ask Luke Weston tomorrow. I've checked his time-table and he's got computer studies fourth period. So guess who's going to be sauntering past the computer room at that time! Gotta be one jump ahead of the Grasshopper!

The Year 7s are holding a sweet stall tomorrow to raise funds as part of this semester's community service project. I told Frog Face I'd help him make some toffee so I'd better go and get him organised.

See ya at school. Don't forget to bring money so you can buy one of our terrific toffees.

Bye.

Rebecca's Recipe for Truly Terrific Toffee

8 tablespoons sugar
4 tablespoons vinegar
2 tablespoons butter

Place all ingredients in a saucepan.
Gently bring to the boil.
Allow to simmer until the mixture turns a golden colour and sets
    when dropped into a cup of cold water.
Pour into paper patties.

You've got to be very careful when pouring the toffee into the
    paper patties, because the mixture is boiling and can give
    you a really bad burn.

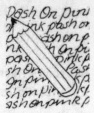

Monday 30th July

Coming home on the bus tonight, feeling the pits, when Chris Asti plonked himself on the seat next to me.

'What's up with you, Rebecca?' he said. 'You look even more miserable than old Weatherby when he's marking the maths papers.'

I kept looking out the window because I didn't want him to see that I was nearly crying. Then he leaned over, rubbed the back of his hand against my cheek and said, 'Hey, Bec, it's me, your old surfing mate. You can tell me.'

And the crazy thing is I did. I told him how I'd asked Luke to go to the school dance and how embarrassed and stupid I felt when he said he was going with Frances Anne Joppa.

'Well, you could always ask me,' he said, leaning back with his hands behind his head. 'You know I refused Frances Anne Joppa just so I'd be available for you.'

'Did you really?' I said.

'Nope,' he said, with that stupid grin of his, 'but I would have if she'd asked me.'

Then before I knew it, everything was arranged. I'm going to the dance with Chris Asti.

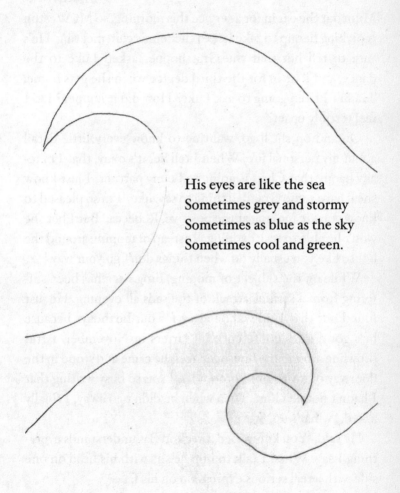

His eyes are like the sea
Sometimes grey and stormy
Sometimes as blue as the sky
Sometimes cool and green.

Tuesday 31st July

Mum put the car in for a service this morning, so Mr Weston is picking her up to take her to the tennis club meeting. He's sure to tell her that the Grasshopper asked Luke to the dance, so I'll be in for the third degree when she gets home: 'Hadn't I been going to ask Luke? How did it happen? Do I feel terribly upset?'

On and on she'll go, wanting to know every little detail about my personal life. When I tell her it's okay, that I'm really happy that Chris is going to be my partner, I just know she'll have some Grandad thing to say, like, 'I'm so pleased to know you are looking at the positive, Rebecca.' But I bet she won't be able to resist adding, 'Instead of moping around the house like you usually do when things don't go your way.'

While on the subject of moping, Frog Face has been suffering from a serious attack of the sads all evening. He just found out that Dad will be away for our birthdays because he's got a sales conference in Surfers in November. After prowling around the house for ages, he came and stood in the doorway of my room. I pretended I was so busy writing that I hadn't noticed him. Then when he didn't go away, I finally asked, 'What's up, Steve?'

He said, 'You know, Bec, I reckon Bas understands everything I say. When I talk to him he sits with his head on one side with a real serious expression on his face.'

I was about to say, 'Well, I don't know about everything, Steve, but he certainly understands "walk" and "ball" and all those words you use to get him to do his tricks.' Then I noticed how Bas was sitting pressed up against Frog Face's legs looking at me with his head on one side and a real serious look on his face.

I said, 'Yeah, of course he does, Steve. After all, Bas is no ordinary dog. He's a percane.'

As I explained that a *percane* was my word for a cross between a dog (a canine) and a person, Bas started wagging his tail furiously and had such a silly grinny look on his face that we burst out laughing.

Wednesday 1st August

Amber's all excited because she asked Gavin if he would go to the school dance with her and he said 'yes' — which of course I knew he would. I told Chris I couldn't understand how Amber could have the hots for that Gavin Spears. 'He's such a moron,' I said, 'I don't know what she sees in him.'

'He's not a moron, Rebecca. In fact, he's a real brain and could easily get the best grades in his year if he wanted to. It's just that he wags classes and goofs off all the time.'

'Well, how smart is that?' I said.

Chris gave me that grin of his and said, 'You can't expect everyone to be handsome, intelligent and charming *and* smart like me, Rebecca.'

I gave him a punch on the arm for being such a pony. He grabbed his shoulder and started groaning and carrying on like I'd really hurt him and everyone in the bus turned around to look. It was *soo* embarrassing.

Thursday 2nd August

Two days since Mum went out with Mr Weston and not a word about Luke not being my partner. I thought that perhaps Mr Weston assumed Mum already knew and didn't bring up the subject, so decided to drop it all casual like as we were doing the dishes. I was sure she would be all concerned and caring, but no, all she said was, 'Well, Chris seems like a nice lad. I'm sure you'll still have a good time.' I mean, my heart *could* have been broken, but she's so wrapped up in her 'relationship' she wouldn't have even noticed.

Wednesday 8th August

Couldn't believe it when Amber arrived at dancing practice in her netball outfit.

'What's with the sports gear?' I asked.

She went all red and said, 'There's no way my mother would let me out if she knew I was going to be with Gavin, so I told her I was going to school for some practice. I just didn't tell her it was to practise dancing for the school social.'

'You're going to look pretty weird turning up looking like a bumble bee in sneakers on the big night,' I said.

'I'm sure we'll think of something before then,' she said, pulling in her belt and hitching up her skirt in a desperate attempt to make Mullun High's black and yellow fashion disaster look a bit more glamorous.

'What's with this *we'll* think of something?' I wanted to know.

'You always have such brilliant ideas, Bec, and as you're my very best friend I know you'll help me to work out something.'

Must say that since Mum has been going out with Mr Weston she's been a whole lot happier. We were laughing and into the girl talk while doing the dishes. I thought it would be a good time to tell her about Amber. She might have some ideas about getting Mrs Satchell to come around. Bad move! She immediately shifted into 'mother mode' and started carrying on about it being wrong of Amber to lie.

'But she didn't *exactly* lie,' I said.

'Leading a person to believe an untruth is just as deceitful as lying, Rebecca. It would be a whole lot better for Amber to be honest and discuss the matter with her parents,' she said.

I pointed out that someone like Mrs Satchell was never going to listen, and if she'd let Amber choose who she wanted to go out with, then Amber wouldn't have to lie.

'That's not the point, Rebecca,' Mum said, banging a saucepan onto the sink.

'Well, that's how much you know, because as far as Amber is concerned that is the point,' I said and stormed out the room.

Now I'm feeling really bad. I feel sorry for Amber but I know what Mum says is right too.

Thursday 9th August

Grandma and Grandad have come to stay for a few days. Grandma brought down a great big box of vegies from her garden and some lemon slice that she had made, and Grandad brought a load of wood so we can have plenty of open fires. He's parked the ute out the front and it's *soo* embarrassing because it's got these bright yellow ribbons tied to the bonnet the way you see on wedding cars. When I asked Grandad about them, he said, 'Well, it's been a while since I've driven in the city, Rebecca, and I thought that some yellow ribbon might help sharpen my sense of direction. Yellow's very good for that, you know.'

Grandma said, 'It's going to take a lot more than a couple of metres of yellow ribbon to help a man who insists on driving the wrong way up a one-way street.'

Grandma's Lemon Slice

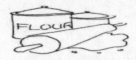

(This is really easy to make and it's just like the lemon slice you
often get in coffee shops.)

1 250 gram packet of Marie biscuits
1 cup coconut
grated rind of 1 lemon
1/2 can sweetened condensed milk
125 grams melted butter

Crush the biscuits to fine crumbs. If you don't have a food
processor, the best way to do this is to put about one-third
of the biscuits in a plastic bag at a time and bash them with
a rolling pin to break them up, then roll them until they are
really fine.

Mix all the dry ingredients in a bowl.
Add the lemon rind, condensed milk and melted butter.
Press the mixture into a greased tin lined with waxed paper.
Top with the lemon icing.
Refrigerate until set, then cut into slices.
Icing
Mix a squeeze of lemon juice, 2 1/2 cups icing sugar and 1
tablespoon of very soft butter until smooth.

Friday 10th August

Grandad wants to buy a computer and he's going to take Frog Face with him to help pick one out, because he reckons that the young ones know more about computers than he knows about growing turnips (which I don't think is a whole lot). He said he wants to get on the net.

'Imagine being able to communicate with a Buddhist monk in a Tibetan monastery, or a Hindu priest in a temple in India, or ...'

Before he could finish, Grandma said, 'Quite apart from any problem you might have with the language barrier, I don't think they're big into computers in Buddhist monasteries or Hindu temples.'

When Grandad said, 'Sometimes you can be quite negative, Philly,' Grandma said, 'You'll find out just how negative I can be if you don't come and give me a hand to cut up the pumpkin. And you can peel the potatoes, Stephen, while Rebecca shells the peas.'

(Grandma's cooking dinner this evening — no prizes for guessing what we're having!)

Saturday 11th August

Frog Face drew up a list for Grandad of the symbols he and his mates use on their emails and mobile text messages. Now Grandad's all excited because he reckons it's going to be the universal language of the future. He says he's going to use it on the net and that eventually everyone in the world will be able to communicate with each other through symbols.

Short message symbols

Smiles (there's a few different symbols): **+D)** =) :-) :)

Unhappy: **=*(** (tear) **:(** (sad face)

lm@	(I am mad)	**M@4u**	(mad for you)	**btw**	(by the way)
+o	(angry or surprised)	**r**	(are)	**tnx**	(thanks)
=p	(tongue out)	**u**	(you)	**wa**	(what)
qt	(cute)	**y**	(why)	**b4**	(before)
4ever	(forever)	**2day**	(today)	**btwn**	(between)
cya	(see you)	**ur**	(your)	**atb**	(all the best)
L8r	(later)	**1-2**	(want to)	**thnq**	(thank you)
g2g	(got to go)	**cul8er**	(see you later)	**ruok**	(are you okay?)
zzz	(time for bed)	**oic**	(oh I see)	**dl**	(download)
c?:	(see?)	**gtg**	(got to go)	**brb**	(be right back)
lol	(laugh out loud)	**hehe**	(laughter)	**///**	(laughing very loud)
pir	(parent in room)	**2fast4u**	(too fast for you)		
afik	(as far as I know)	**fyi**	(for your information)		
bcnu	(be seeing you)	**wru**	(where are you?)		
pcm	(please call me)	**peg**	(song, sound, music)		

8 is really useful because you can use it to make so many different symbols:

h8 (hate)   **d8** (date)   **m8** (mate)   **l8** (late)   **gr8** (great)

urxlnt (you are excellent)	**w8ing4u** (waiting for you)	**f2t** (free to talk)
yz (wise)	**sz** (size or sighs)	
cu@7 (see you at 7)	**b/curqt** (because you are cute)	

We asked Mum and Grandma if they could think of any other symbols. Mum came up with some pretty ordinary stuff that she uses at work, but Frog Face added them to the list anyway.

eg (for example)	**ie** (that is)	**vip** (very important person)
asap (as soon as possible)		**aka** (also known as)

rsvp (which is French shorthand for *repondez s'il vous plait* — answer if you
please, which means you've got to reply to an invitation)

24/7 twenty four hours a day, seven days a week

Grandma came up with some good ones:

mt (empty)	**gg** (horse)	**swak** (sent with a kiss)

swalk (sent with a loving kiss — for really special people)

From: 'Rebecca' rlarking@hotmail.com
To: 'Amber' am-chatting@hotmail.com
Subject: What a gas!
Date: Sunday 12th August

Mum, Grandma and I have just come back from a walk. We had to get out of the house or we would have died. Grandad offered to cook this evening and he made a curried vegetable dish with loads of lentils and all sorts of beans in it. It was really delicious, but boy, did it have a bad effect on some people! Ever since dinner Grandad's been farting, Frog Face has been farting, and worst of all Basil — who got to eat the leftovers — has been farting. (When we were out walking Grandma let go a couple too, but Mum and I pretended not to notice.)

From: 'Rebecca' rlarking@hotmail.com
To: 'Amber' am-chatting@hotmail.com
Subject: Five-minute hero
Date: Thursday 16th August

You won't believe it. You just won't believe it. Frog Face is a hero, a five-minute hero.

He was going to take Basil for a walk after school, but Basil stopped in front of Miss Featherston's and refused to budge when Frog Face called. He just sat there whining and scratching at the fence. When Frog Face went to drag him away he heard someone calling for help. He climbed over the fence and found Miss Featherston sprawled out on the ground. It seems that Napoleon got stuck up the liquid amber tree and Miss Featherston tried to climb up after him, and fell and broke her hip.

Frog Face called an ambulance for Miss Featherston and rescued Napoleon from the tree. Now she thinks he's the greatest thing since plastic wrap. She sent him a humungous box of chocolates as a reward.

I've tried not to eat too many in case I break out in pimples and Mum's on a diet, so Frog Face has been having a real pig-out. Even though Mum told him that chocolates aren't good for dogs, he sneaked a couple to Basil. He reckons Bas deserves to share the reward.

Gotta go and get stuck into my science assignment.

See ya tomorrow.

Saturday 18th August

    Mum's gone to the pictures with John Weston.

    Frog Face is in the bathroom chucking up.

    Basil is moping around the house looking seedy.

    There's more snow on our television set than on Mt Kosciusko.

    Amber's got to stay home and study.

    Sometimes I feel I'm just hanging around waiting for my life to start but nothing's happening.

From: 'Rebecca' rlarking@hotmail.com

To: 'Amber' am-chatting@hotmail.com

Subject: Five-minute hero

Date: Saturday 1st September

Amber, you've got to check out the *Mullun News*. You know how the newspaper runs this series called 'Local Heroes'. Well, Frog Face was chosen as the hero of the week. Plastered across the front page there's this photo of him with Basil sitting at his feet with that stupid grinny look he gets when you tell him he's a good dog. Splashed across the top of the photo there's this big headline that says 'Local Boy and His Dog Save Woman and Rescue Pet Cat'. Frog Face is trying to act all cool, but you can tell he's really pretty pleased with himself.

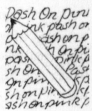

Sunday 2nd September

Mum told Miss Featherston she thought it was really nice of her to nominate Frog Face as a Local Hero.

Miss Featherston said, 'Oh, Mrs Larking, I only wish I could take the credit for being the one who put Stephen's name forward, but I must confess that I was so distressed at the time that it didn't occur to me.' Then she said, 'Perhaps it was that nice young ambulance driver or one of the nurses.'

Mum said, 'Perhaps.'

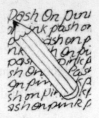

Tuesday 4th September

I thought that when Dad left nothing would ever hurt me again. But I was wrong. I feel as though I have swallowed an enormous stone and it is stuck in my chest. I can feel it there all the time, cold and hard.

It always seemed that no matter what happened both Grandma and Grandad were always there for us, that other things changed but they didn't. So when we got a phone call early this morning from Grandad to tell us that Grandma had died of a heart attack, I couldn't believe it. I still can't believe it.

When Mum got off the phone she started to cry. Awful, sobbing crying that made her whole body shake. It really frightened me. I went and put my arms around her and said, 'Don't cry, Mum,' but she shouted, 'She's my mother and she's dead. I'll cry if I want to.'

Frog Face was sitting on the couch with Basil, tears streaming down his face. It was awful. I wanted to say something to him, but couldn't because I was crying too. After a while Mum came in and cuddled us both and said she was sorry she had yelled and we sat on the edge of the couch hugging each other.

As soon as Dad heard that Grandma had died he came around. He brought a couple of casseroles and a cake. Gloria must have made them, but instead of giving us the usual 'Look what Gloria's done for you' bit, he just gave them to me and quietly said, 'Pop these in the fridge, Rebecca. Your mother probably won't feel like cooking just now.'

He was really terrific with Mum. Sat talking gently to her while she cried. He said he'd drive us to Grandad's and help with the funeral arrangements.

As he was leaving, he gave me the biggest hug and said, 'I'm relying on you, Rebecca, to let me know if your mother needs anything.'

I realise now that even though we don't live in the same house any more he's still my Dad and he really does love us and will always be there for us.

Friday 7th September

It was Grandma's funeral today. I'd never been to a funeral before and was feeling really freaked out about it. I thought it would be spooky and weird. I was scared that I was going to see Grandma's body and I didn't know how I'd cope if I saw someone dead.

But Dad told me that the coffin would be closed during the service. He said some people like to see the person they loved one last time, but they usually go to the funeral parlour to do that. Grandad went but Mum and Stephen and I didn't want to.

The funeral was sad, but it's really strange, there was also a sort of peacefulness about it. Grandad gave a speech — Mum said it is known as an eulogy. He was wearing a suit that looked like it was three sizes too big for him. Mum said

Grandad never had much use for a suit, so it was probably the one he had for her wedding. When he stood up in the pulpit, he looked like some scared little kid on his first day at school. For a minute I thought he was going to lose it, but then he straightened his tie — he was wearing a magenta satin tie, the colour of the spirit — and he was okay.

He told how he'd met Grandma when he was seventeen and she was sixteen and that they had been married for nearly fifty years. He said that after such a long time their spirits had become so entwined that when she died a part of him died too, but there was also a part of her that lived on in him, Mum, Stephen and me.

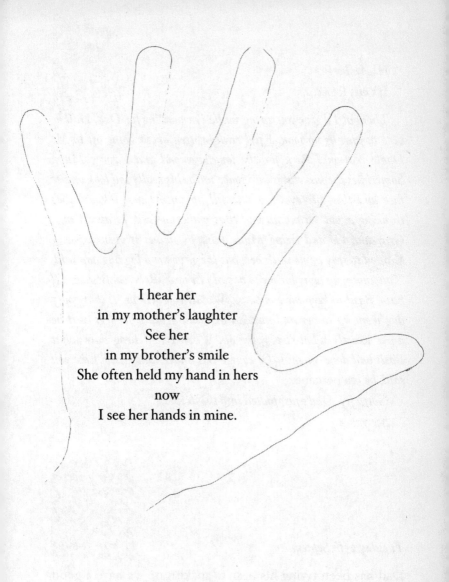

I hear her
in my mother's laughter
See her
in my brother's smile
She often held my hand in hers
now
I see her hands in mine.

Hi Amber!
It's me, Rebecca.

Thought I'd give you a ring while I'm waiting for Dad. He'll be here to pick us up soon. I feel really rotten about going off to Mt Dagle National Park for the long weekend and leaving Mum. Sometimes she just stares into space with this really sad look on her face and then her eyes begin to fill up with tears. I know she's thinking about Grandma and that makes me sad, because I miss Grandma too and seeing Mum unhappy makes it even worse. I wanted to stay home with her, but she gave me a big hug and said, 'You know, it's okay for me to be sad just now, Rebecca. Besides, I'll have Basil to keep me company.' Would you believe it, that goofy dog went up to her and nuzzled his head against her legs as if he knew exactly what was going on. When I told Frog Face what Basil had done, he said, 'Of course Bas understands, Bec. Like you said, he is a percane.

Gotta fly. Dad's just pulled into the drive.
See ya!

Tuesday 25th September

Dad has been trying his best to make sure we have a good time. Up at the crack of dawn and dragging us down to the beach for an early morning surf. Playing frisbee and cricket on the sand with Frog Face and the Kid, BBQing enough food to feed the entire campground. This morning he decided we should climb Mt Dagle to watch the sunset. Gloria said she'd prefer to stay back at the cabin and catch up on some reading. I don't think she's into sweaty activities that might make her make-up go streaky. Frog Face and the Kid wanted to do the Twilight Animal Spotting Walk with the rangers, so it was just Dad and me.

When we got to the peak it was like being on top of the world. We sat with our backs resting against this enormous granite boulder and watched the most brilliant sunset I've ever seen. The sun was like a huge slice of watermelon and as it disappeared below the horizon the sky turned all gold and pink and crimson. Even though it was really beautiful, I still felt all achy and sad inside. Dad must have sensed how I was feeling because he asked if I was okay. I told him how I kept thinking about Grandma, wondering what happened to her after she died and how I wished I knew that she wasn't lonely and unhappy.

Dad said, 'Do you know what makes a sunset, Rebecca?' I told him how we learnt in science that it was the light from the sun reflecting on tiny particles of dust and stuff that were floating about in the atmosphere. 'And the sun, where did it come from?' he asked.

I told him, 'Nobody knows that.'

Then he put his arms around my shoulders and said, 'It's quite beyond our comprehension, isn't it, Rebecca. And you know, I think that's how it is with Grandma. Even though we know what happens to a person's body when they die, we don't know what happens to their spirit. I'm sure it's like the sunset, something quite wonderful even if it is beyond our understanding.'

From now on, whenever I look at a sunset I'll think of Grandma.

Silver tears at sunset
Golden smiles at dawn
Life gives us songs and laughter
And a time to mourn.

From: 'Rebecca' rlarking@hotmail.com
To: 'Amber' am-chatting@hotmail.com
Subject: Local hero
Date: Friday 28th September

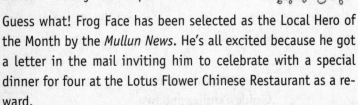

Guess what! Frog Face has been selected as the Local Hero of the Month by the *Mullun News*. He's all excited because he got a letter in the mail inviting him to celebrate with a special dinner for four at the Lotus Flower Chinese Restaurant as a reward.

'And who are you going to take as your guests?' Mum asked, when he showed her the letter, like she didn't think for one moment it wouldn't be her.

Frog Face said, 'I'd like to take Dad.'

'Oh! Well, I'm sure your father and Gloria will be absolutely delighted if you ask them,' Mum said in this terribly bright voice with this tight little smile stretched across her face.

'But I want you to come, Mum, you and Dad and Rebecca, the four of us, just like it used to be.'

'Stephen, I'm sorry, but you've got to understand that it's just not going to work like that any more. Things have changed with your father and me, and now that he's with Gloria he naturally wants to take her when he goes out.'

When Frog Face said, 'But I don't want Gloria to come instead of you,' Mum said, 'Why don't you ask one of your friends? Or perhaps you could ask Miss Featherston. Now that would be a really nice thing to do.'

There are times when you just can't believe the sort of stuff that mothers come up with. Well, of course Frog Face wasn't too impressed with that idea and said, 'I'll take Basil. After all, he's a hero too.'

Mum started to get annoyed. 'Don't be ridiculous, Stephen. You know you can't take a dog to a restaurant.'

Frog Face said, 'Well, I'll take a doggy bag and bring his meal home for him.'

Then Mum got really cross. 'Sometimes I don't know what gets into you, Stephen. You're old enough to realise I've got enough to put up with without this sort of carry on.'

Frog Face stormed out the kitchen and locked himself in his bedroom with Basil.

When Mum called him for dinner he wouldn't come out for ages, but Bas kept scratching at the door because he didn't want to miss out on his bowl of dog food.

Eventually Frog Face did join us, but announced, 'I'm only here because Bas needs his dinner.'

It was really great, Mum sitting at the table heaving and sighing, Frog Face making these disgusting slurping noises as he ate, and Basil snuffling into his bowl.

Saturday 6th October

Mum went out with Mr Weston tonight. She was running late as usual, so I had to show him into the lounge room. Frog

Face and Bas sat directly opposite him, just staring at the poor man. It was *soo* embarrassing.

Finally, Frog Face said, 'So you and Mum are going out tonight?' then made this funny little noise in the back of his throat, which is really a signal for Bas to do his growling and baring his teeth trick.

Mr Weston didn't seem to notice. 'Yes, Stephen, we're going to see the local repertory group's performance of *The Importance of Being Ernest*.'

Then Frog Face said, 'Mum always tells us that it's not a good idea to have a late night during the week,' then gave Bas the signal to growl again, and Bas again obliged.

'Well, I don't expect it will be a very late night, Stephen,' Mr Weston said.

Frog Face was silent for a bit, then he came out with, 'Mrs Williams took our class for science today.'

Mrs Williams is the biology teacher and usually gives the sex education lessons to the Year 7s. I thought I would die, I really did, wondering what Frog Face was going to say next. Thank goodness Mum walked in at that moment.

'Oh, I see you've been having a nice little chat,' she said in this bright voice.

'Yes, you could say we've been getting to understand each other a little better,' said Mr Weston with a funny grin.

When Mum left, I said to Frog Face, 'If Mum finds out what you and Bas were up to she's going to kill you.'

I thought Frog Face would tell me to rack off, but instead he went on about how he was just trying to look out for Mum and that whenever he tries to do something nice he ends up in trouble.

I didn't want him cracking the sads all evening, so I said,

'How about we make some chocolate crackles?' Frog Face is such a garbage guts that any offer of food cheers him up immediately.

Now he's yelling something about not being able to find the copha, so I'd better go.

We couldn't make chocolate crackles because we didn't have any copha and we had run out of paper patties. So I told Frog Face I thought we could make something even better. When my slice turned out to be really scrummy I said to Frog Face that the true test of genius was the ability to turn a potential disaster into a success. Frog Face said that with all the disasters that happen at our place one of us was bound to end up winning the Nobel Prize.

Scrummy Chocolate Crackle Slice

4 cups rice bubbles
1 cup coconut
2/3 cup cocoa
1 1/2 cups icing sugar
250 grams butter

Mix rice bubbles, coconut, sifted cocoa and sifted icing sugar in a
    large bowl.
Melt the butter, pour it into the bowl and mix well.
Press into a well-greased slice tin and refrigerate.
When set, cut into slices.

I reckon if you used only three cups of rice bubbles and added
    about a cup of nuts or dried fruits and some little
    marshmallows it would be even more scrummy.

Wednesday 10th October

We had dancing practice after school again tonight. I must say, old-fashioned dancing has got a lot going for it. You get to dance close to your partner, *real* close.

During the break I went to the toilets and, wouldn't you know, the Grasshopper swans in after me.

'It's just wonderful having Luke for a partner,' she said, fluffing out her hair then gazing into the mirror like she was about to kiss herself. 'It's a pity you've had to make do with Chris Asti.'

'As it happens, Frances,' I said in my snootiest voice, 'I'm really pleased I'm going with Chris. Not only is he good looking *and* the junior surf champion but he's one of the *nicest* people I know.'

Funny thing, it wasn't until I said it that I realised it was true.

Thursday 11th October

Amber's been in a bad mood nearly all week. At first, whenever I asked what was wrong she'd just say, 'Nothing.' Finally I said, 'I bet it's because of that Gavin. He's been coming on too heavy, hasn't he?'

She said, 'He's not like that, Rebecca, and if you'd only give him a chance you'd find out that he's a really nice person.'

'Whatever,' I said. 'But if it isn't Gavin, what is it then? You've been such a sack of sads lately.' As soon as I said that I felt really awful, because her eyes filled up with tears. I put my arms around her and said, 'Why don't you tell me what's wrong? I tell you everything.'

After a while she told me that she was worried about her end of term report.

'So! What's the worry?' I asked. 'You always get good results.'

For a minute I thought she was going to start crying again. I just couldn't believe it when she said, 'But I won't get all A's, Bec, and that's what Mum wants. She reckons that I'm not putting in enough effort and that I'll never get into any worthwhile uni course when I finish school if my grades don't improve.'

I told Mum all about it while we were doing the dishes. 'What is it with Mrs Satchell, that she's putting so much pressure on Amber?' I said. 'I mean, it's not as if she's been slacking off or anything and she's doing really well.'

All Mum said was, 'Well, Rebecca, it seems like I'm not such a bad mother after all.'

What is it about parents? When you don't want to know what they think, they're full of advice. When you really would like to know, they go off on another beat.

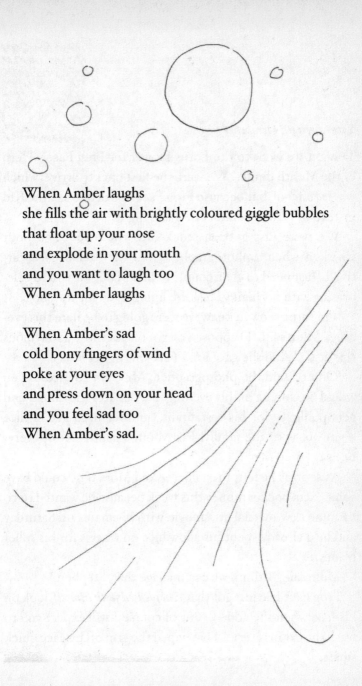

When Amber laughs
she fills the air with brightly coloured giggle bubbles
that float up your nose
and explode in your mouth
and you want to laugh too
When Amber laughs

When Amber's sad
cold bony fingers of wind
poke at your eyes
and press down on your head
and you feel sad too
When Amber's sad.

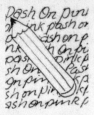

Saturday 13th October

Tonight we went to the Lotus Flower for Frog Face's Hero of the Month dinner. We were the first ones to arrive, which was *soo* uncool, but because Frog Face decided to ask the Kid instead of Dad, it couldn't be a late night.

We were just getting stuck into the Sweet and Sour Chicken when a photographer from the *Mullun News* arrived. 'Just need to get a couple of pics of our local hero celebrating with his family,' he said, lining us up for the shot.

'I'm surprised you knew we were going to be here this evening,' Mum said. 'I suppose you got one of those anonymous tips again.' And she gave Frog Face one of her looks.

'Oh no,' said the photographer. 'Mr Chin advised us you would be coming in this evening. He donates the dinner and gets publicity for his restaurant, and our hero gets a nice night out with the family. Everybody's happy! Now, everyone say "fried rice".'

As soon as he left, Frog Face asked Mum if he could have some extra pocket money this week because he wanted to go to some new martial arts movie with his mates on Saturday and he'd already spent his allowance on wheels for his roller blades.

Mum said, 'I think we can manage that, Stephen.'

Frog Face had just got that *real pleased with himself* look on his face when she added, 'But of course I will expect you to wash the car in return.' That wiped the grin off his face quick smart.

Pretty Smart Dim Sim Soup

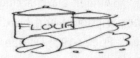

Sometimes Mum makes this soup. It's really quick and easy to make, it tastes great, and it looks just like the one you get in a Chinese restaurant (sorta).

To a can or prima pack of chicken stock add a couple of chicken stock cubes and enough water to make up to one litre.

Bring the chicken stock to the boil and drop in a packet (about 15) of mini dim sims.

Simmer until the dim sims are cooked (usually about six minutes).

Beat an egg with a fork, then slowly pour it into the soup mixture, making sure you stir the soup all the time so you get these long shreddy bits of egg through the soup.

Add some chopped spring onions (the green part).

Stir through and serve immediately.

(I told Mum that Grandma had shown me how to make chicken stock by simmering some chicken bones with about three litres of water and a couple of chopped onions, a sliced carrot and a celery stalk. She would throw in some salt and peppercorns, parsley stalks and a bay leaf and let it all simmer for a couple of hours. Then she would strain it and put it in the fridge until the next day, when she would skim the fat off the top. It's dead easy, but Mum says she hasn't got time for that sort of thing when she's working.)

From: 'Rebecca' rlarking@hotmail.com
To: 'Amber' am-chatting@hotmail.com
Subject: Victim of horrible disease
Date: Friday 19th October

Have you got purple spotted lumps and a scabby green rash too?

Are your eyes all yellow and popping out, your tongue turning navy blue?

Is your nose melting off your face and dripping orange goo?

Are you covered in sores that are oozing puss that smells like doggy poo?

I think you must have caught the Plague and the Black Death too,

For it's been one whole day since I've heard from you.

Rebecca speaking.
Oh, hello Mrs Satchell.
No, I don't know where Amber is.
Really, Mrs Satchell, I promise I don't know. We've been here with Dad all weekend.
Sure, if I hear from her I'll tell her.

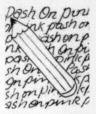

Sunday 21st October

When we got home from Dad's, Mum was in the garden looking like a great big green sweat ball. She told us she had spent the entire day weeding and digging and pruning.

'And what's brought about this sudden interest in horticulture?' I asked her.

When she said, 'Gardening is a very therapeutic activity, Rebecca,' I said, 'And this therapy wouldn't have anything to do with a certain school teacher who's been calling around lately, would it?'

She just gave a bit of a grin. 'Well, I did think that it was time to make an effort to get the place looking decent again.'

Mum said she was too exhausted to even think about cooking, so we got to have fish and chips in front of the telly. But even though the gorgeous Shane was in a coma, I couldn't concentrate on *Life in Double Vale* for thinking about Amber. Mrs Satchell said Amber had gone to the library just before lunch but hadn't come home. I felt pretty sure that she had gone sneaking off somewhere with Gavin but couldn't understand why she hadn't emailed me all weekend.

Next thing the doorbell rang. It was Amber's parents. They wanted to know if I was sure I didn't know where Amber was. I told them I hadn't seen her since school on Friday. Mrs Satchell started off in that 'all nice' sort of voice that adults use when they are really mad at you but are trying not to show it.

'I know that you and Amber are the most wonderful

friends, Rebecca,' she said, 'and I'm delighted that she has someone she can trust and rely upon, but often friends cover up for each other out of a sense of loyalty, and sometimes that loyalty can be misguided.'

All the time she was talking she kept on smiling and pretending to be all friendly like, then she went on to say, 'While I respect the fact that you may not wish to break Amber's trust, I'm sure you'll understand that we are very worried about her, so if you have any idea where she is it is most important that you tell us, Rebecca.'

I said, 'Honestly, Mrs Satchell, I *don't* know where Amber is.'

Mr Satchell, who is really nice, asked me, 'Do you have any idea at all where Amber might be, Rebecca?'

So I told them again how I'd sent Amber some emails but she hadn't replied and she hadn't rung me either.

'And you can't think of anywhere where she might have gone?' he asked.

By this time I was getting sick of them asking all these questions and treating me like I was hiding something. 'Like I keep telling you,' I said, 'I don't have a clue where Amber is.'

Then Mrs Satchell said in this really *horrible* voice, 'I find that very hard to believe, Rebecca.'

I put my hands on my hips and said, 'Well, you can believe what you want.'

That's when she really lost it and started screaming, 'Don't you go lying to me. I know you two are as thick as thieves and I know you're a part of this.'

Mr Satchell tried to get her to calm down, but she just kept on yelling at me. I could feel my face going all red and my eyes all hot, but there was no way I was going to cry in front of her. I was about to say, 'Why don't you go around and start yelling at Gavin Spears?' when Mum said, 'I realise you are upset, Mrs Satchell, but I will not stand by and have you call Rebecca a liar. If she said she doesn't know where Amber is, she doesn't know. I promise that if we do hear anything we will contact you straightaway. In the meantime, I think it would be better if you left.'

Monday 22nd October

Some kids reckon that the cops are mean because they're always telling you off for riding skateboards in the shopping mall and stuff like that, but the police who came to school this morning were really ace.

They said it was important that anyone who had seen or heard anything that might help with finding Amber come forward. Then they spoke to me alone.

'You think something bad has happened to Amber, don't you?' I said and started to cry. The policewoman put her arm around my shoulder and told me she was sure Amber would be okay. She said that sometimes kids who'd had a fight with their parents cleared out, and she wanted to know if I thought that might have happened with Amber.

When I said I didn't know, the policeman asked if there was anyone else who might know where Amber was. I told them that the only other person was Gavin Spears. They said Mrs Satchell had already given them his name and they had spoken to him, but they didn't think he knew anything about Amber's disappearance.

If Mrs Satchell and the police weren't enough, at lunchtime I had Frances Anne Joppa sidle up to me and ask, 'Is it really true that you don't know where Amber is?' I just stared at her, because I couldn't believe that she could be so thick, then she said all prissy like, 'Because if you do know, Rebecca, I think you should tell.'

Well, I did this big act of pretending to look around to make sure that no one could hear, before I said, 'Of course I know where she is, Frances.' Then I leant towards her and whispered, 'And I'll tell you if you promise not to say a word to anyone.'

Well, the Grasshopper's eyes almost popped out of her head.

'She's hiding under my bed,' I said. For a second the Grasshopper stood there with her mouth flapping, and then she realised I was having her on and got all snooty.

'I'm serious, Rebecca Larking,' she said. 'Although I can't understand why she would want to hang out with someone like you, I like Amber, and I do want to help. So would you tell her from me that running away ... well, it doesn't solve anything.'

'And just what would you know about it, Frances Anne Joppa?' I asked.

The Grasshopper just stood there looking at me for a minute, her face going all red, then she walked off.

That girl is such a pain.

After school I raced around and found Chris and told him I wouldn't be going home on the bus because I had something important to do.

Gavin hadn't been at school all day. I had a fair idea where he would be and that there was a chance that Amber might not be too far away. Sure enough, I found him hanging outside the Jump 'n Rock Cafe.

When I went up to him, he said, 'Well, if it isn't Princess Poop Doesn't Stink.'

I wanted to snot him one but somehow managed to keep it cool. I told him that everyone was getting really worried about Amber and that even though he had told the police he didn't know where she was I reckoned he did. He looked me in the eyes and said, 'Read my lips, Rebecca. I don't know where Amber is. In fact, I've been here at the mall all day looking for her.' I had been so sure he knew something I had to bite my lip to stop myself from crying. As I started to walk away, he called out, 'Rebecca, if I find out anything I'll let you know.'

Amber, wru?

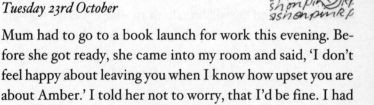

Tuesday 23rd October

Mum had to go to a book launch for work this evening. Before she got ready, she came into my room and said, 'I don't feel happy about leaving you when I know how upset you are about Amber.' I told her not to worry, that I'd be fine. I had to study for a maths test in the morning.

But there was no way I could concentrate on studying. I

was so worried about Amber. I kept thinking of all the dreadful stories about young girls who had gone missing and checking to see if she had sent any emails or text messages.

I'd just finished writing my diary and was hopping into bed when there was this scratching noise on the window. I thought it was someone trying to break in. I was so scared and my heart was beating so fast that I thought I might die. Then this voice said, 'Rebecca, it's me, Amber!' I could hardly believe it! As I jumped out of bed she said in a loud whisper, 'Don't turn on the light. I don't want anyone to see me.'

We managed to pull off the fly wire screen so she could climb inside. She looked really bad, all dirty, and her eyes were red and puffy like she had been crying a lot. She smelt a bit wiffy too, but I didn't care. I gave her the biggest hug. I was so pleased to see her. We wrapped ourselves up in my doona, because she was all cold and shivering, and sat huddled together on the bed.

'Amber, where've you been? What happened?' I asked.

'She never leaves me alone, Bec.'

Even though I guessed who she was talking about, I said, 'Who?'

'Mum. She found out that I'd asked Gavin to the school dance and we had this most humungous fight. She told me I could just go and 'unask' him, because there was no way she was letting me go anywhere with him. Then she started raving on that it was probably because of his bad influence that I wasn't doing as well at school as I should and that I'd better start and concentrate on my studies instead of wasting my time with some no-hoper like Gavin Spears. I couldn't take it any more, Bec. I needed some space so I just took off. I walked for hours and hours. I didn't know where to go or what to do, but no way was I going back home. Then her voice went all shaky like she was going to start crying. 'You don't know what it's like, Rebecca. Your parents are cool. Gavin is the only one who really understands.'

'What do you mean, Gavin understands?' I felt a bit hurt that Amber didn't think I would understand.

'Well, he keeps getting it from his parents too. His father's a doctor and his mother lectures at the uni. They keep putting pressure on him to become some hot-shot lawyer or scientist. And that's not what Gavin wants to do. He told them he wants to be a music teacher — although what he really wants is to have his own band. His parents went right off. They reckon that being a music teacher is just a waste. Gavin reckons if he can't do what he wants, he's not going to bother trying to get good marks. That's why he goofs off in class and skips school.'

'Did he know where you were?' I wanted to know.

'No, of course not. And the only reason I didn't tell you was because I knew everyone would think you were in on it, and I didn't want to get you into trouble.' And she gave me another smelly hug,

Amber told me that she wandered around until it got dark, then went to the back of the supermarket and crawled into a couple of crates and covered herself with cardboard boxes. She was in the middle of telling me how a couple of really rough guys and this girl came along and they were drunk and she was scared of what might happen if they realised she was there, when all of a sudden the bedroom door burst open. Frog Face came charging into the room swinging his cricket bat in the air and yelling, 'Get away from my sister or I'll bash your brains out!'

For a while it was total confusion — Frog Face doing his hero to the rescue bit, Basil bounding about the room yelping and barking, Amber crying, and me screaming, 'Put the bat down, Steve. It's okay, it's only Amber!'

Because we had sat up talking until late, I didn't wake up at the usual time. Mum came to tell me to get up and when she saw Amber curled up in bed beside me she rushed across and wrapped her arms around her.

'Oh Amber,' Mum said, 'I'm so glad you're safe. We've all been frantic.' Then she turned around and started yelling at me. 'I trusted you, Rebecca. I can't believe that you could be so irresponsible! I would have thought that when the police became involved you would have had enough sense to realise things had gone too far.'

Amber was crying again but somehow managed to blurt out, 'Don't blame Rebecca, Mrs Larking. She didn't know anything about it until I came around last night.'

By this time Frog Face had appeared at the door. 'It's true, Mum.'

Mum cooled down then, but when she said, 'We'd better ring your parents straightaway,' Amber got all upset.

'What if you go and have a shower while I make myself a cup of coffee,' Mum said. 'And I promise I won't call your parents until we've had a little chat.'

While Amber was under the shower Mum rang Mr Weston, who said that he thought the best thing for Mum to do was to take Amber to the school counsellor. He said he would ring Amber's parents and tell them to meet there.

Amber didn't want to go at first, but eventually Mum convinced her that she had to sort things out with her parents. 'I think you know that they really do love you, Amber, and I'm sure that if you all go and talk things over with a counsellor you'll be able to work it out.'

We were just about to leave when I remembered the maths test. 'I'm going to be at least half an hour late,' I wailed. Mum rang Mr Weston again and he said he'd sort things out with Mr Weatherby.

When I finally got to school, Mr Weatherby said he was very pleased to hear that Amber was safe and well and not to worry about the maths test. I said, 'Does that mean I don't have to do the test now, Mr Weatherby?'

He said, 'No, Rebecca, that's not what I mean at all. I will set another test just for you and you can stay in after school one evening and do it while I'm marking some papers.'

I should have known better than to expect *him* to be nice.

Thursday 25th October

Whenever Mum wants to have a 'little talk' with you, she waits until you're in the car, travelling along at about 60 kilometres per hour, so there's no possible hope of escape.

This time we were on our way to the library. 'Now, Rebecca,' she said, 'you're not to go asking Amber about her sessions with her parents and the school counsellor. If Amber wants you to know, she'll tell you herself, so don't go prying and certainly don't go making remarks about Mrs Satchell. 'Even if you think she can be a little ... well, too strict at times, you must remember that she is still Amber's mother and I'm sure she's only been doing what she thinks is best.'

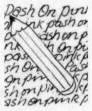

Friday 26th October

Grandad is staying with us for a couple of days. Yellow ribbons must have more power than I thought, because he only lost his way once, which is pretty amazing seeing as he didn't have Grandma to guide him. As I started to write that last bit, I could almost hear him saying, 'Grandma's always there to guide me, Rebecca.' He must miss her so much. I know I do.

I told Grandad that Dad said he would have something exciting to show us next weekend. Mum said, 'I can't imagine what it could be. That household already has every appliance and gadget known to humankind.'

As I went out the room, I heard Grandad say, 'He is the children's father, Jennifer. You shouldn't run him down in front of them.'

Mum started off all indignant. 'All I said was, "I can't imagine what it could be".'

But Grandad wasn't letting go. 'You know very well it wasn't so much what you said as the way you said it. It is important for the children to know that you and Dave loved each other very much when you married. That is a truth that cannot be altered because of what happened between you later.'

Before Mum could say any more, he said, 'I'm just going to

pop in to see Elsie Featherston. She has been very kind to me.'

'Kind!' I heard Mum squawk. 'What do you mean, kind?'

I didn't hear Grandad's reply as I had to duck into my room before he came out. Just for a joke, I later asked Mum if Grandad and Miss Featherston were going to be an item, but she got really cranky and said, 'No, they are not. I don't know how you could imagine such a thing, Rebecca.'

Saturday 3rd November

Mum cooked a roast for dinner. The potatoes were beyond crispy and the meat was dry, but it's important to encourage her, so Frog Face and I told her it was terrific. We even had dessert. Frog Face was into his second helping of ice-cream with warm caramel sauce when she said, 'I got the credit card statement today. It was quite a shock.' Before I could say, 'What else is new!' she went on to say that, as much as she would like to be able to do something really special for our birthdays, she hoped we wouldn't mind sharing a celebration. Frog Face went on scraping the pattern off the bowl and said, 'That's okay by me.'

I just kept staring at her without saying a word. I couldn't believe that she would even think of suggesting that I would want to celebrate *my* birthday with my *kid* brother.

But she totally ignored my look of horror and went on to say, 'I thought you might like to take a friend each to the Luxury Lounge Cinema. I'll arrange for you to be served popcorn and soft drinks.' I still hadn't said anything. She glanced at me and added, 'I could probably even stretch to pizza.'

Frog Face pushed away the bowl and said, 'Ace. Is there any more dessert?'

Never Fail Caramel Sauce

2 tablespoons butter

3/4 cup evaporated milk

1/2 cup white sugar

1 1/2 cups brown sugar

Place all ingredients in a saucepan, place over a low heat and stir
until the sugar dissolves.

Simmer until thickened (approximately 5 minutes), stirring
occasionally.

TV dead.

Will u record Life in Dble Vale 4 me pls

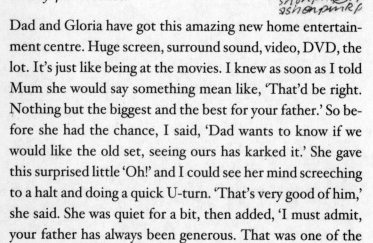

Sunday 4th November

Dad and Gloria have got this amazing new home entertain-
ment centre. Huge screen, surround sound, video, DVD, the
lot. It's just like being at the movies. I knew as soon as I told
Mum she would say something mean like, 'That'd be right.
Nothing but the biggest and the best for your father.' So before she had the chance, I said, 'Dad wants to know if we
would like the old set, seeing ours has karked it.' She gave
this surprised little 'Oh!' and I could see her mind screeching
to a halt and doing a quick U-turn. 'That's very good of him,'
she said. She was quiet for a bit, then added, 'I must admit,
your father has always been generous. That was one of the
things I liked about him.'

Frog Face has invited the Kid to the pictures next Saturday. He's got three really good mates and he didn't want to
choose just one. I'm glad now that I'm only having Amber,
because I don't want my other friends to know that I have to
share my birthday celebration with Frog Face.

Saturday 10th November

Birthdays are special. Birthdays are fun. Your birthday is the day when you get to do all the things you want to do, and your family and friends make a big fuss of you, and you get wonderful presents and surprises. This year I had the best birthday ever — NOT!

First of all, Mum announced that as it was Frog Face's birthday on Thursday and mine on Saturday she would cook a special family celebration meal for us on the Friday. (Obviously we overdid the praise bit when she made a roast dinner the other night.) Thank goodness Friday turned out to be one of her 'You wouldn't believe what it's been like at work' days. Frog Face and I managed to convince her that we wouldn't *really* mind if we had takeaway chicken and chips and it *would* be okay if she bought us a double cream sponge birthday cake with chocolate fudge frosting from the bakery instead of baking one herself.

Mum gave me a gorgeous lace bikini briefs and bra set. I think the bra is a bit big, which confirms my suspicions that I must be the most flat-chested girl at Mullun High.

Frog Face gave me a family-size block of chocolate, but I can't eat it because I'm getting another pimple on my chin. It looks like it's going to be humungous. It will probably end up being bigger than my boobs.

Dad called from Surfers and asked if Frog Face and I liked

the portable CD players he'd given us. Since we hadn't yet opened the parcels, it rather spoilt the surprise.

I got some gorgeous scented candles and aromatherapy oils from Amber. I left the candles near the heater and they went all soft and droopy. The oils are divine, Sensitivity and Harmony, but I've just read the labels and they are described as a combination of fragrances to promote feelings of tranquility and to fill the mind with the glow of generous thoughts. Now I'm beginning to wonder if she is trying to tell me something.

Frog Face really liked the tee-shirt and sneakers from Mum and thought the Swiss Army knife I gave him was ace. He took it to the pictures to show the Kid. A theatre attendant saw him flicking it open and was going to call security. I managed to convince the manager that Frog Face was a local hero, not some brain-dead moron who was planning to slash the seats, and he agreed to hold the knife until we were leaving. I'd just got that sorted when the Grasshopper and some of her gang came in to buy tickets for the evening show. It would have been total humiliation if they had seen me going to a matinee with a couple of kids. I left Amber hiding behind a life-size cardboard figure of Russell Crowe, while I raced into the toilets and hid in one of the cubicles. Wouldn't you know, the Grasshopper and her gang came in to fuss up their hair. I crouched up on the toilet seat — one glimpse of last season's purple and red sneakers underneath the toilet door and she would have known it was me. She was talking about Luke. Something about him being a great kisser but I couldn't quite catch what she was saying. I leaned towards the door while still standing on the seat, lost my balance, crashed down and had to scramble up onto the seat again.

One of her gang called out, 'You okay in there?' I flushed the toilet and at the same time squeaked, 'I'm fine, thank you,' so they wouldn't recognise my voice. They stayed tittering and giggling for ages. By the time they went, the film had already started and the theatre was dark. I couldn't see where the others were sitting and when I whispered 'Amber' everyone shushed me. If that wasn't embarrassing enough, I knocked over the Coke that was set up on the little table next to my seat and had sticky brown liquid running down the leg of my jeans.

Saturday 10th November
Dear Grandad
    I had to write straightaway to thank you for the birthday present. It is so very special.
    When Steve and I came home from the pictures, Mum said, 'There's one last birthday surprise for you both.' I knew as soon as I saw the blue paper and orange ribbons that the parcels were from you. When I opened my present and saw Grandma's silver and moonstone necklace I couldn't believe it. I remember her telling me that you gave it to her when she was a young woman. It was the most wonderful gift you could ever have given me. I will treasure it forever. Thank you so much.
Lots and lots of love
Rebecca

PS Steve loves the bird book that was Grandma's. We didn't know that she had won a prize for identifying and imitating bird calls.

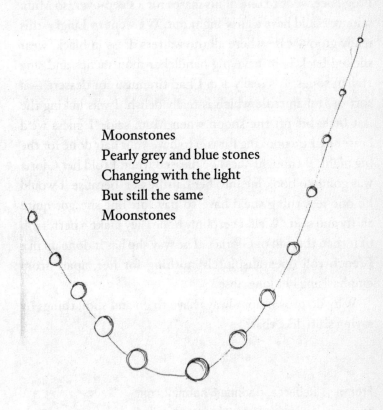

Moonstones
Pearly grey and blue stones
Changing with the light
But still the same
Moonstones

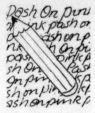

Friday 16th November

Frog Face went to one of his mates for a sleep-over, so Mum said we could have a girls' night out. We went to Luigi's, this really groovy cafe where all the waiters dress in black, wear slicked-back hair, have big handlebar moustaches and sing Italian songs. It's really ace. I had tiramusu for dessert — a sort of Italian trifle which is really delish. I was licking the last little bit off the spoon when Mum said, 'I guess we'd better make a booking for you to have your hair done for the big night.' I thought she'd be pleased when I told her Gloria was going to book me into her hairdresser, because it would be one less thing she'd have to pay for. But she got quite sniffy and said, 'Well, I certainly hope they make a better job of it than they do of Gloria's. The way she has it done up in a French roll does absolutely nothing for her, apart from emphasising her long nose.'

Why do grown-ups always have to go and spoil things by saying stuff like that?

From: 'Rebecca' rlarking@hotmail.com
To: 'Amber' am-chatting@hotmail.com
Subject: Guess who's coming to dinner?
Date: Saturday 17th November

Have just got in from doing the big supermarket shop with Mum — guess who's coming to dinner?

Mum said, 'What if we pick up the ingredients for your spag and meat sauce? You could make it for dinner. I'll do the dessert.'

'You'll do dessert?' I wasn't sure that this was going to be such a great deal. My mother's idea of dessert is ice-cream and tinned fruit, or a Sara Lee pie for the special occasion meal.

'Yes, I'll do the dessert,' she said in her 'I don't know why you sound so surprised' voice. 'Gloria isn't the only one who can whip up a decent pud, you know.'

I asked what she was going to make, but she said it was a surprise, which is a bit of a worry.

She lashed out and bought dinner mints and some fancy cheeses and even tossed a couple of cans of Bas's favourite dog food into the shopping trolley instead of the brand that was on special. Things must be going really well with Mr Weston!

Sunday 18th November

I wasn't looking forward to last night but it turned out to be okay.

I'm glad Mum and Mr Weston didn't go behaving all soppy, because the thought of Mum being with someone else feels really strange. Frog Face managed to behave himself and even Basil didn't do anything disgusting like licking his private parts or dragging his bottom along the carpet like he does when someone he doesn't like comes around.

I asked Frog Face how come he'd been a regular little ray of sunshine during dinner. He told me that he had been chatting to Grandad on the net and Grandad asked what he thought of Mr Weston. 'I told him he was pretty cool and Grandad said not to go embarrassing Mum and spoiling this friendship for her. Besides, Mr Weston has got to be a whole lot better than someone like that slimy Mr Purvis from the tennis club you were always going on about.'

Mr Weston thought my spaghetti and meat sauce was about the best he had tasted. Mum's dessert, which turned out to be tiramusu, was really delicious. She told Mr Weston that I'd enjoyed the tiramusu so much the night we went to Luigi's that she pleaded with Luigi to part with the recipe — which she believed had been passed down from his old Italian grandmother.

When Mum and I were in the kitchen clearing up the dinner dishes I told her I didn't think old Italian grandmothers would be in to using White Wings Instant Pudding.

She said, 'Take if from me, Rebecca, some of those Italian grandmothers were extremely inventive.' I told her I thought some Australian mothers were extremely inventive too.

Soo good Tiramusu

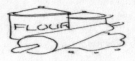

1 packet sponge fingers
300 ml cream
300 ml milk
1 packet White Wings Instant Vanilla Pudding
1 cup cold black coffee
1/2 cup marsala or boronia
300 ml extra cream
vanilla essence
1 teaspoon icing sugar
powdered chocolate

Add the marsala to the coffee.

Beat the instant pudding mix with 300 ml of cream and 300 ml of
milk until thick and fluffy (two to three minutes).

Line a bowl with sponge fingers that have been dipped in the
coffee mixture.

Cover with half the custard mixture.

Add a second layer of sponge fingers that have been dipped in
the coffee mixture.

Spread with the remaining custard.

Stand in the fridge overnight.

Before serving, whip the extra cream with icing sugar and a few
drops of vanilla essence.

Spread the cream over the top of the dessert and sprinkle with
powdered chocolate.

Monday 19th November

Mum asked me how Amber and her parents were getting on with the school counsellor.

'You told me I wasn't to go asking Amber about her counselling sessions, and look who's doing the prying now?' I said.

'I was merely showing my concern for Amber,' Mum said, putting on her hurt voice. 'However, if you think I'm prying I won't bother asking again.'

I said, 'Come on, Mum, you know you just love to hear about everything that's going on.' Before she could say anything else, I told her that Amber said things were a lot better at home and that her parents had agreed to allow Gavin to take her to the school dance. When I told Mum that Mrs Satchell couldn't believe that Gavin's father was a doctor and his mother a uni lecturer, Mum said, 'Well, I've no doubt that that bit of information helped change her attitude towards Gavin quite a bit.' I don't think Mum likes Mrs Satchell much.

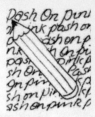

Tuesday 20th November

Exams start next week. Mum keeps saying stuff like:

As long as you do your best, that's all that matters.

We all have to face challenges in life.

I don't know what you're worrying about, Rebecca.

If you spent your time studying instead of worrying, you'd be better off.

Believe it or not, Rebecca, the world won't stop turning if you happen to fail a couple of exams.

I wish she would say something original that would make me feel better.

When I was chatting to Grandad on the phone tonight, he said, 'Rebecca, all knowledge dwells within us. We only have to tap into it.' Only problem was he was a bit vague about how you turn on the tap.

Exams.
Dark monsters
that grow more terrifying as they draw closer.
I attack them with my pen,
assault them with words,
wrestle them with my mind.
Some bits I cannot grasp
mock me.
'I'll get you next time,' I yell
as they disappear into the future,
their high-pitched laughter
ringing
in my head.

From: 'Rebecca' rlarking@hotmail.com
To: 'Amber' am-chatting@hotmail.com
Subject: Bird watching
Date: Wednesday 21st November

Must say dancing lessons haven't quite been quite the same without you hopping around in your bumble bee netball uniform. Hope Gavin grows his hair back before the big night. Bald eagle tattoo on a bald head is not a good look. Are you quite sure it is only one of those wash-off jobs?

Frog Face reckons he's inherited Grandma's talent for doing bird calls. He has spent hours practising. His pigeons sound like they need a packet of throat soothers, but his kookaburra and wattle bird are pretty good. Napoleon has been sitting on the fence gazing up at the trees with a puzzled look on his face all afternoon.

See ya tomorrow

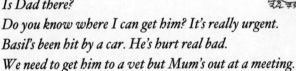

Hullo, Gloria!
It's Rebecca.
Is Dad there?
Do you know where I can get him? It's really urgent.
Basil's been hit by a car. He's hurt real bad.
We need to get him to a vet but Mum's out at a meeting.
Will you? We'll be out the front waiting.

Monday 26th November

Basil has his leg in plaster but the vet said he'd be frolicking around like a puppy in no time at all.

Got to give it to Gloria — she was pretty terrific, considering the way Frog Face and I have been treating her.

While we were waiting for the vet, she put her arms around Frog Face and didn't seem to mind that he was blubbering all over her good blouse, making it grubby with his dirty face and snotty nose. She even paid the vet's bill and bought us both an ice-cream on the way home.

Mum agreed that it would be nice to do something to thank her, so Frog Face and I are going to bake some muffins for her.

Rebecca's Marvellous Choc Chip and Orange Muffins

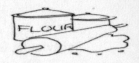

(makes about eight Frog Face sized muffins or ten regular
  muffins)
1 1/2 cups plain flour
1/2 cup sugar
2 teaspoons baking powder
1/2 teaspoon salt
1/2 cup melted butter
1/2 cup orange juice
2 eggs
grated rind of one orange
3/4 cup chocolate chips

Sift the flour, salt and baking powder into a bowl.
Add the sugar and mix lightly.
Melt the butter, add the orange juice, orange rind and eggs, then
  beat together.
Stir the orange mixture into the flour and sugar. (Stir gently so
  your muffins will be nice and light.)
Spoon into greased muffin tins.
Bake in a moderate oven 180°C / 350°F for 15–20 minutes.

Frog Face has just shown me the list of advice he's drawn up for Bas.

Behavioural Guidelines for Basil Larking

Don't wag your tail near the coffee table.

Don't bury your bones under the couch cushions.

When you do bury your bones outside, don't spend half the night barking at the possums. They aren't planning to dig up your bones.

Don't look so pleased with yourself when you've rolled in something disgusting.

Walking away from the bowl of leftovers Mum puts out for you is not a good move.
Remember, we all have to eat her cooking.

When everyone grabs their nose and says, 'Oh phew! Who made that dreadful smell?' sniffing behind the TV isn't going to fool anyone.

It's no use pretending you're asleep and can't hear Mum telling you to get off the couch if you go and wag your tail when she says 'Isn't he cute' (even if it is a mean trick).

Have a different way of greeting each member of the family: face licking for Stephen, tail chasing for Mum and barking and jumping for Rebecca. That way everyone thinks they're special.

When Mum says you are not to be fed tidbits from the table, just look pathetic and she'll soon give in.

There's no need to go lying with your head between your paws, looking miserable, when you see good-looking dogs doing stunts on telly. It is probably trick photography and, besides, looks aren't everything.

And whatever you do, *don't* go racing after Napoleon when he stalks across the road. There's probably a car coming.

Saturday 1st December

They announced the Local Hero of the Year in the *Mullun News* today. The man who rescued the young girl who had been swept out at the surf beach got the award. I thought Frog Face would be really disappointed, because the winner gets a night at the Hilton Hotel and tickets for two to the test cricket.

'I guess you feel a bit disappointed about missing out on the big prize,' I said.

But Frog Face just said, 'Nah! I didn't want to win anyway.'

I said, 'Come on, Steve, getting presented with a bat signed by the Australian cricket team and having the chance to meet the captain — you would have thought that was ace.'

Frog Face said, 'If I had won, I would have wanted to invite Dad because he loves the cricket and Mum isn't a bit interested. But if I did invite Dad, then Mum would have got all hurt.' Then he said, 'You know what I hate most, Bec? It's feeling like you've got to pick between them.'

I said, 'Don't be such a stupid dork, Steve. Mum and Dad don't want you to choose between them.'

Frog Face stood there scuffing his feet for a minute, before he blurted out, 'They say they don't, Bec, but that's what it feels like sometimes.'

I've gotta admit I do know how he feels.

Wednesday 5th December

Went to Mullun Mall with Mum after school. Got this really gorgeous dress to wear to the school dance — baby blue with little shoestring straps — and a pair of strappy white sandals with some money Dad had given me.

Grandad really loves it when we ring for a chat, so I gave him a call to tell him how gorgeous Grandma's necklace looks with my new dress. I told him how I was looking forward to the end-of-year social but I felt a bit sad too because it meant that the school year would be over. Should have seen one of his little meditations on life coming. This time it was, 'Rebecca, while it is important to have goals and destinations in life, it is equally important to enjoy the journey.'

From: 'Rebecca' rlarking@hotmail.com
To: 'Amber' am-chatting@hotmail.com
Subject: Disaster
Date: Monday 10th December

The *worst thing* you can possibly imagine has happened.

I should have known it was going to end up being a whole lot more than a bad hair day the moment Frances Anne Joppa got on the bus and cast her poppy eyes around until they lobbed on me.

'You needn't bother sitting there,' I said, as she plonked herself next to me, 'that seat's taken.'

'I don't think so, not if you're saving it for Chris Asti,' she said in her snooty little voice. 'In fact, from what I've seen and heard I'd say you'll be sitting all on your own-some in future, Rebecca.'

One part of me wanted to choke her until she told me what she was rabbiting on about, the other part wanted to play it cool because I didn't want to give her the satisfaction of thinking that I was even remotely interested in anything she had to say. But of course I didn't have to decide between strangulation and hypothermia because she just couldn't wait to blab.

'I guess it will be pretty hard to get another partner for the school dance at this late stage,' she said with this really smug look on her face.

Even though my stomach was getting more knotted by the minute, I said real casual like, 'Why would I want to do that, Frances? Chris is going to be my partner.'

Of course now I realise that's exactly the sort of remark she wanted me to make, because she could hardly wait to say, 'Oh really. I would have thought that now he's back with his old girlfriend, Kelly Rivers, he won't be wanting to take *you* to any dance.'

That's when I lost it. 'What do you mean?' I demanded.

'Oh, don't tell me you didn't know!' said the Grasshopper, putting her hand up to her mouth and pretending to be all shocked. 'I wouldn't have dreamt of saying anything if I'd realised. But, on the other hand, perhaps I'm doing you a favour by telling you.' She grabbed her bag and stood up. 'After all, we wouldn't want him two-timing you and making you look a fool, would we, Rebecca?' And she flounced off.

I keep going over all the times Chris and I have been together and I can't believe he'd do such a thing. Mum's been asking me if there's anything wrong. In the end I told her I was really tired because we had been training for the school swimming carnival. She said in that case I'd better have an early night, so I've gotta go.

See ya tomorrow.

Tuesday 11th December.

Got this poem in the mail from Grandad. It's really nice, but doesn't tell me a thing about what to do when I come to a River.

Life is taking you on a journey.
Travel light,
you don't need excess baggage.
Face the direction in which you are going,
instead of looking back at where you've been.
Try not to complain when the way is bumpy,
others will be having a rough ride too.
Don't be afraid to ask for directions,
if you're feeling lost.
Make joy, love and loyalty your companions,
kindness your guide.
And make sure you ring home,
often.

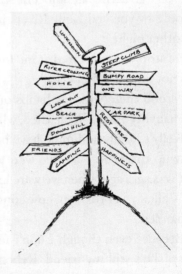

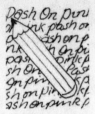

Just when I thought things couldn't get any worse, they did. I had been avoiding Chris and frantically trying to think of someone else I could ask to partner me to the dance. Then I was going to tell Chris I didn't want him to take me, so it would look like I dumped him, instead of the other way around. I was hurrying to catch the early bus when Chris caught up with me. He draped his arm around my shoulders and started talking like nothing was wrong. I was so angry. I shrugged him off and said, 'You needn't feel obliged to be nice to me, Chris Asti, just because you *were* supposed to be taking me to the school dance.'

'What are you talking about?' he asked.

'Don't go acting all innocent with me,' I said. 'The whole school saw you and Kelly Rivers in Cosmos Coffee Lounge the other night.'

He stopped and stared at me for a minute, before he said, 'It's not like that, Rebecca.'

I stood there with my hands on my hips and said in this real haughty voice, 'Well, then, what *is* it like?'

'Kelly's family and mine have been friends for years. We grew up together. Sure, we were an item at one stage, but that was ages ago, when we were kids.'

'Well, if you broke up, how come you're still seeing her?' I demanded.

'Because even though I don't feel *that* way about her any more, she's still my friend, Rebecca, and I still think she's cool.' Then he said, 'And if you'd bothered to ask me instead of listening to what other people say, I would have told you that.' And he walked off.

Thursday 13th December

I bombed out today, was late for maths and Mr Weatherby carried on like I had committed the crime of the century. Ms Iser gave me a blast because I forgot to bring my assignment for science and then I got into trouble during English because I wasn't paying attention. But I couldn't stop thinking about what I was going to say to Chris after school.

He was talking with a group of boys near the oval, so I walked by and casually said, 'Hi Chris.'

He said, 'Hi Rebecca,' and kept on talking. I had to sit on the fence and wait for ages before he came wandering up.

I said, 'I need to talk to you, Chris.' He stood there, not saying a word the entire time I was telling him how I sorry I was and that I should have known better than to take notice of what someone else said about him, particularly when that person was Frances Anne Joppa. I said that I was sure that Kelly Rivers was a nice person and I was glad he didn't go slagging off about her just because they weren't an item any more. Then I said I hoped that things could be the same between us again. For a moment he just stared into my eyes. I could feel my face getting all hot and my eyes starting to burn, because I was sure he was going to tell me to get lost.

Then he leant over and kissed me. It was the best kiss yet and made me feel all jelly-like in the tummy.

Now I'm lying in bed writing my diary, thinking about everything that's happened and what Chris said about him and Kelly, and I realise it's a bit the same with Mum and Dad. I guess things changed for them too, but I'm glad they still get along.

I just hope that Kelly Rivers doesn't go hanging around Chris too much.

Friday 15th December

Tonight was girls' night in. Amber came over and it was into the beauty treatment. We'd gone halves in a bottle of nail polish so it was Pash on Pink fingers and toes all round. Mum decided she needed all the help she could get, so had to get in on the act too. She told us that egg white made a really good face mask. After spreading the slimy gooey stuff on each other's face, we were supposed to let it dry without moving a muscle. We must have looked like three mournful clowns sitting on the couch staring straight ahead while our faces shrunk into this hard white mask. Basil wandered in, took one look at us, yelped and raced into Frog Face's room. Well, that cracked us up, literally.

When Mrs Satchell came to collect Amber, she was all gushy and nice, but I could tell she still doesn't like me. Who cares! Tomorrow night I'll be dancing with Chris until dawn. (Well, until midnight.)

Don't think I'll be able to sleep a wink with the excitement. But if I don't get my beauty sleep, I'll end up with black rings under my eyes. Will try counting the number of times Chris will have to kiss me before my Pash on Pink lip gloss wears off!

Saturday 16th December

Last night was just awesome. I had the best time. When I got all dressed up and looked in the mirror I couldn't believe it was really me. Even Frog Face said I looked okay — which is about as high as you can go on his compliment scale.

When Chris Asti arrived, my heart did this funny little flip-flop — just like you read about in books. He looked *soo* hot all dressed up in a jacket and red tie and I could tell by his eyes that he thought I looked pretty good too.

Just as we were about to leave, the doorbell rang. It was Dad.

'Your carriage is waiting, princess,' he said, sweeping his arm through the air.

Parked in the drive was this amazing white stretch limousine. Gloria and the Kid were sitting up in the front waving and grinning. 'Come on, there's room for everyone,' Dad said to Mum.

While Frog Face was saying, 'Oh, wow! I bet we'll be the only ones to arrive in a limo,' Mum wasn't saying anything. But I knew she was thinking, 'Why does he always have to go for the biggest and the best?' For a minute I was afraid she was going to say she'd take her own car, but then she turned to Dad and said, 'I'll just go and grab my bag.'

When we got in the limo, Gloria went on about how pretty I looked and how handsome Chris looked, then she told Mum she looked nice too.

'Why thank you,' Mum said. I could hardly believe my ears when she went on, 'And I must say how lovely your hair looks, Gloria. You should wear it up in a French roll more often. It really suits you!'

The hall looked great, all decorated with streamers and balloons in the school colours. First up we did some of the dances that we had been taught, but after the dinner it was relax and groove the night away.

There I was having a really good time dancing with Chris while Dad was busier than a Hollywood film director with his new video camera, Frog Face and the Kid were working their way through the desserts, Gloria was all smiles, and Mum was laughing and talking with Mr Weston.

Amber looked gorgeous in this pink frothy-looking dress, and even though Gavin had dyed his hair blonde and looked a bit like an albino porcupine Mrs Satchell was so busy talking to Dr and Mrs Spears that she didn't seem to notice.

I was just thinking that everything was working *soo* well when Frances Anne Joppa waltzed by with Luke Weston and I had this really horrible thought. If Mum gets together with Mr Weston and Frances Anne Joppa ends up with Luke Weston, I'll be related to the Grasshopper!